THE WONDERFUL WINTER

Other books for young people by
MARCHETTE CHUTE

AN INTRODUCTION TO SHAKESPEARE
THE INNOCENT WAYFARING

E-P-DUTTON & CO.INC
OVER 100 YEARS OF CREATIVE PUBLISHING
EST. 1852

FINSBURY
FIELDS

MOOR FIELDS

The Curtain   The Theatre

SHOREDITCH ROAD

The
Wonderful Winter

By MARCHETTE CHUTE

Illustrated by
GRACE GOLDEN

E. P. DUTTON & CO., INC.

NEW YORK

Library of Congress Catalog Card Number: 54-8857

For
Elizabeth Marchette Smith
and
William Frank Smith
from their admiring aunt

The action of this story takes place in the reign of Queen Elizabeth the First, between the autumn of 1596 and the spring of 1597.

Chapter 1

Sir Robert Wakefield had a fit of the wiggles.

One difficulty was that he had on his best suit of clothes, the black velvet with the silver embroidery. The black velvet was hot and the embroidery tickled his neck. Sir Robert had been carefully brought up and it was unthinkable that he should scratch his neck, but he thought of it nevertheless. He raised his hand tentatively toward his collar and then caught the eye of his eldest aunt. At once he put his hand back into his lap again.

The other difficulty was that dinner was lasting much longer than usual. Never had there been so long a time between the beef and the tarts. It seemed probable that time had ceased altogether and that some form of eternity had taken its place. October would become November, November would turn into Christmas, and still the five of them would be sitting there while his collar strangled him slowly.

His three aunts did not usually linger over their dinner, especially in the autumn when there was so much to be done in the great house. But today his tutor had arrived, and the conversation had been intellectual. At least, Sir Robert felt it must be intellectual. It made very little sense to him.

"One of our great masters of philosophy," said the tutor. "I knew him well at Cambridge."

"Take a little more of the mustard," said Aunt Isabella, and motioned to have the pickles passed again.

Next to the dais on which they sat, the windows were small and high. They framed the warm, golden sunlight of an autumn afternoon, while within Sir Robert sat as quietly as possible for one who is being slowly suffocated by black velvet.

He had been hopeful about the new tutor. With winter coming on and the great gray house turning chill and lonely, he would be someone to talk to during the long evenings while the three aunts embroidered. He might even be willing to take a few walks in the woods and be shown the place where the foxes sometimes came on snowy afternoons.

Then the tutor arrived and Sir Robert knew that he had been mistaken. He was too polite to let himself think that his new tutor looked like a rat, but he had once met a rat who looked exactly like his tutor. The rat had appeared in the long grass suddenly, next to a stalk of meadowsweet, and glared at him. There was the same thin nose and underslung jaw and the same bright, darting eyes, and if the rat had had a rather wispy beard the resemblance would have been really striking. The tutor was not a comfortable-looking man and it was clear he would not be interested in the kind of winter that Robert had in mind.

The tarts came and remained. The conversation continued, endless and incomprehensible. And then, all at once, his Aunt Isabella said, "You may go now, Robert."

He got up from the table quickly in case she should change her mind. He bowed deeply to each of them, as he had been taught to do, and Aunt Eleanor gave him her soft, rather vague smile. But no one reached out to give his hair a friendly ruffle as he left the dais, and certainly no one thought to kiss him. He had never been kissed by any of his aunts as far back as he could remember.

Once, when he was perhaps six or seven, he had a nurse named Meg. She was fat and given to laughing and she did not call him Robert. She called him Robin and tickled him frequently, and he followed her about wherever she went. Once she went south on a visit to her family and he could not follow her there, but when she came back she had a present for him. It was a sheaf of ballads she had bought at a penny apiece, and he could still remember his excitement when he unwrapped the package and saw the thick black lettering and the gay, bold pictures. There was one about Mother Watkins's Ale and one about the Kind Widow of Watling Street. There was the burning of Beckles town, and a monstrous pig, and an earthquake, and the lamentations of the ladies of Troy, and all of them had splendid illustrations. He and Meg fastened them to the chimney piece in the nursery, and she promised to teach him the tunes as fast as he could learn them.

The ballads stayed on the chimney piece for one day only. Aunt Eleanor found out about them and told Aunt Bertha, and Aunt Bertha told Aunt Isabella. The next day they were all gone, even the monstrous pig, and the next week Meg was gone, too. She said her sister needed her at home, but she was crying when she left.

Robin did not cry, since he did not have a sister as an excuse. But he managed to save a small part of the pig, charred from the kitchen stove but still quite monstrous, and he kept it safe in the small box that held his father's signet ring.

Robin did not remember his father, but the painting in the great hall of the fair young man with the sword looked too young to belong to any relative of his dark-robed aunts. Nor did he remember his mother, for she had died three weeks after the news came that her husband had been killed in a battle at sea. Whenever Robin could not sleep at night he would fill in the time by trying to imagine what she had been like. He felt she must have been very beautiful and he hoped she had been happy.

Outside in the courtyard the October sun lay warm on the paving stones and the woods beckoned. But Robin had on his best clothes, and he knew he was expected to stay fairly close to the house.

Perhaps there would be no objection if he went and stood quietly by the river to watch for the kingfisher. The kingfisher had been coming to the same spot for five days now and it was just beginning to get used to Robin. Moreover, it was the kind of occupation that would leave him with his head clear in case the tutor started asking him after supper what he knew about Latin verbs.

Robin stationed himself carefully on the clean grass by the river and waited, but the kingfisher did not come. It had been an unlucky day from the beginning. Robin stared somberly at the water, chewing on a long piece of grass.

There was a faint ripple where the sun caught a movement near the reeds, and Robin's interest quickened. It might be an otter.

The ripple became a splash and the reeds quivered. Robin

stayed very still, his breathing so quiet that not even the oldest and wisest of otters could detect him.

The splashings became more violent. It was certainly not an otter.

Something wet and brown came into view. It shook itself violently, standing so close in the shallow water that the drops sprinkled Robin's black velvet. He did not notice. He was staring enchanted, and then he put out a coaxing hand.

A small spaniel clambered up the bank, slipping a little in the mud. "Oh, dog!" said Robin softly, and dropped to his knees. His hand remained outstretched, but the spaniel did not need it. He knew well enough when someone loved him. He gave a single leap and landed, safe and muddy, in the circle of Robin's arms.

"Oh, dog!" said Robin again, his voice shaking with delight. The spaniel reached up out of his cradling arms and joyfully licked his ear. Then he licked his face with equal thoroughness, and Robin bent his head and hugged him close.

He had never had a pet. Aunt Isabella said that they were untidy and a waste of time. The only animals that ever came into the house were the long-legged beasts that leaped among the trees and flowers in the embroidery frames, and no one can pet a unicorn or make friends with a lion made of embroidery silk.

Once, at harvest time, Robin had found a nest of field mice in one of the wheat fields. The little round nest had hung on a thistle until it was trampled down by the boots of the men. Robin gently pried it open, drawing aside the neatly plaited blades of wheat, and found eight little mice, naked and blind. There was nothing he could do for them except to hang the nest carefully on a whitethorn hedge, out of the way of the harvesters' boots, in the hope that the parents would find it again. But perhaps if he had been allowed to bring the baby mice home and feed them with warm milk, he might have been able to raise the whole family.

He had once tried it with hedgehogs, when he found a litter at the north end of the kitchen garden. The milkmaids believed that hedgehogs sucked the milk of the cows and killed any they could find, so it was a family of young orphans that Robin discovered. They were difficult to pet because they had stiff little bristles on their sides and backs, but Robin visited them every day for a week. He brought them beetles and they flourished. Robin always thought of them as his own hedgehogs, but he knew that they really were not. They were garden animals and probably would have been just as happy if he had never met them.

"Oh, little dog," said Robin, holding his cheek against the feathery ears, and the spaniel whimpered for joy.

The important thing was to introduce the idea to his aunts gradually. If he could get the puppy up to his room and wash and brush him thoroughly, perhaps they might be very pleased to have a spaniel in the house. After all, spaniels were lap dogs as well as hunting dogs and many ladies owned them. If the dog were looking his best, and if Robin's aunts had time to get used to the idea . . .

Robin got up and unbuttoned the front of his doublet. He was luckily rather thin, and if the dog clung tightly to his shirt there was no reason why he could not reach his room quietly and unseen. The front hall was always rather dark, and the servants were well trained and not inquisitive.

He made a safe entrance through the front door, moving quietly but trying not to look furtive about it. He had thought of whistling, to show how calm he was feeling, but had to give up the idea because his lips were too dry. A few servants were working at the lower end of the hall, putting the silver plate back into the court-cupboard. But they did not look up and Robin reached the staircase in safety.

His foot was on the first step when he heard a voice behind him.

"Sir Robert!"

Robin turned and saw the tutor smiling at him. At least his lips were smiling, but his eyes were not.

"Sir Robert, you seem to be in a great hurry. Not in too great a hurry, I trust, to answer a few questions about your Latin."

Robin was thankful that the hall was so dark. He half turned so that he would be leaning against the newel post. Then he said politely that he would be glad to answer any questions that the tutor wished to ask him.

"What is the Latin for *furtive*, Sir Robert?"

"*Furtivus*," said Robin.

"And for *futile?*"

"*Futilis*, sir. Or *inanis*."

"*Inanis* will do. And what, Sir Robert, is the Latin word for *tail?*" He smiled again, but still not with his eyes.

Robin did not dare look down at his doublet. But he could feel a rhythmical thumping against his ribs, not so quick as the beating of his heart but exactly what a small spaniel might be doing with a small freed tail.

"*Cauda*," said the tutor softly. "*To wag the tail: caudam movere*. I would suggest you put the animal on the floor."

Robin stood motionless, and the tutor reached over and loosened the puppy from his shirt front. He set him on the stone floor where he sprawled, affable and muddy, and

looked up at them both. The tutor wiped his fingers delicately.

"I shall inform your aunt," he said.

Robin waited, his hand on the newel post and the puppy on the floor in front of him. He did not trust himself to look down.

Somewhere a door opened and closed and Robin could hear the tutor's voice raised in explanation. For a moment he had a wild hope, and then he lost it when he saw the face of his eldest aunt. She was rigid with anger but not at the tutor.

"Robert," she said, "you will go to your room at once. We shall not expect you down for supper."

He turned and went, since there was nothing he could do that would not make the matter worse. He had reached the first landing when he heard his aunt's voice behind him. She was speaking to one of the servants and her voice was still rigid.

"Tie it up by the stables," she said. "I will have it disposed of in the morning."

Chapter 2

Robin sat on the edge of his bed and stared down at his shoes. He was not supposed to sit on his bed because he might damage the gold embroidery on the coverlet, but for once he did not care.

It was not so much that he had lost the little dog. He had not had a dog yesterday, and he could learn to live without a dog tomorrow. Other people managed to live that way, even after they had stroked a pair of soft spaniel ears and knew what it felt like.

It was what his aunt had said that frightened Robin. She should not have used a word like *dispose*. That was the same word she had used when Meg's ballads had been taken down from the wall, and the ballads had been burned. It was of course foolish to think that Aunt Isabella would hurt a little dog, but she could be unkind without meaning to be. She had already called the dog "it," as though he were some inconvenient kind of stick that Robin had brought in from outside and carelessly left in the hall, and no one had said anything about feeding him.

Perhaps, after the house was dark and all the candles and torches were out, Robin could creep downstairs and give the little dog his supper. He would pat him and tell him not to be afraid, that everything was going to be all right.

Robin's fingers dug into the gold embroidery. It was not

going to be all right. There was no knowing what was going to happen in the morning.

He sat motionless on his bed, staring at the open window. The tree just outside moved its leaves restlessly in the small wind that had come up. There would probably be rain before morning.

On the other side of the house the sun had begun to slip down behind the hill.

Robin suddenly got up off the bed. He began to unfasten himself from his best clothes, his embroidered doublet, his slashed breeches, his shoes with the rosettes and his long knitted stockings fastened with the silk points. He piled all his clothes, neatly folded, on a stool and then began padding about the room in his shirt and bare feet.

He went to the bed, rolled back the heavy coverlet and slid one of the pillows out of its case. The pillowcase would make an excellent bag for carrying things in, and he looked at it with quiet satisfaction as he laid it out tidily on the floor.

Then he went to the carved oak chest where he kept his clothes and took out an old leather jerkin and some heavy brown breeches. They had been patched but there was much wear in them yet, and he would need the warmest pair he owned with winter coming on.

He hesitated between two pairs of shoes. The Spanish leather fit him better, because they were his newest pair and his feet had been growing lately. On the other hand, the English leather would be less likely to let in the rain and the snow. After a moment's thought he pulled on a pair of heavy stockings and tried on both pairs of shoes, walking gravely around the room to see how they felt. He expected to be doing a great deal of walking and his feet were going to be important to him. Finally, after giving the matter much thought, he kept the shoes of Spanish leather on his feet and put the English ones inside the pillowcase. He would take them both.

After that things went more quickly. He brought out all his shirts and added them to the shoes, along with a kind of quilted waistcoat that he had always found comforting in cold weather. To this he added all his stockings, since he did not know how to mend them when they wore out. He put his comb on the pile, and then after some thought added his soap dish. It would be easier for the puppy to eat out of a dish than from the bare ground.

Robin dressed himself carefully, his eyes searching the room for anything else he might need in his travels. He strapped an old leather belt around his waist and slipped into it the small knife with which he made his pens. Then he filled his wallet with various small things he did not wish to leave behind. This included his father's signet ring and the scrap he had been able to salvage from the ballad of the monstrous pig. There was also an old coin he had once found on the landing. He had left it there for two days after he found it, in case its owner should come and pick it up, and after that he decided that it belonged to him.

He found his old black woolen cap in the cupboard where he had stuffed it last spring and brushed it off carefully. It had a heavy lining and would be useful for carrying water in, or even milk if they should find a cow. Also, it would keep his head dry if it rained.

Then he went over to the smaller chest, where his schoolbooks and writing materials were kept. He brought out two sheets of paper, a rough one for his first draft and a smooth white sheet for the fair copy. He set up his inkhorn and goose-quill pen and licked the nib of it thoughtfully, rubbing it against the inside of his coat to soften it while he thought what to say.

It was no easy matter to tell his three aunts he was running away. He tried four different ways of opening the subject, and each of them seemed more undutiful than the last. Finally he decided not to mention the matter at all but just to leave them his good wishes.

On the smooth white paper, and in his best hand, he carefully wrote the final draft of his letter.

> Dear and honored ladies,
>   Do not worry about me and the dog. We will be all right. I wish you long life and every happiness.
>   Your respectful nephew,
>   Robert Wakefield

He put an extra curl on the W and sealed the wax with his father's ring. Then he put the letter in the middle of the bed, where it could not be missed, and weighed it down with his silver shoeing-horn.

Then he picked up the pillowcase to see how much it weighed. It was going to make an awkward sort of bundle, especially when he had added some food to it, but as soon as he reached the woods he could cut himself a stick and carry it slung over his shoulder.

He did not know how late it was, but he had been working for some time by candlelight. Even if he waited half the night, he would still have no assurance that some stray servant might not be stirring about. He tucked his bundle under his arm, blew out his candle and started for the door.

Then he stopped and took off his shoes, wedging them

under one arm with his elbow. His clothes were fortunately dark and he knew how to move silently, because he had followed many birds and animals through the woods. It should not be impossible to slip into the kitchen and out again without being seen.

The house was still and a dim white light was coming through the windows. Robin was sorry to see that. A boy and a dog could easily be seen by moonlight. On the other hand, it would be easier to find the puppy out by the stables, so perhaps it was all for the best.

In the kitchen there was a strong, steady glow from the banked fires, and Robin hesitated in the doorway. If anyone came in suddenly he would be seen. On the other hand, it was useless to start on his journey unless he could collect enough food to last two or three days at least.

He slid along the wall, keeping to the shadows and alert to flatten himself out if he heard footsteps. Once he heard a scuffling and stopped still with his heart beating hard. But it was followed by a small, irritable squeak, and Robin knew it was only a mouse. His Aunt Isabella would not be pleased to know there were mice in the kitchen.

When he reached the chopping table at the far side of the kitchen he found the reason for the mice. Someone had set out a little midnight supper, with the remains of a cold joint of beef, a loaf of rye bread and a wedge of cheese.

Robin had been dreading the idea of trying to grope his way into the dark larder. He did not know where anything was kept and he was sure to step on a crock and set it rolling. Here was enough to last him for two days at least, and he stuffed it into his pillowcase with a light heart. It did not really belong to anyone, and there was plenty more in the larder for anyone who wanted supper at midnight. He hur-

ried, for the light of the great fireplaces was full on him, and
then he slid out the kitchen door.

There was a gray cloud near the moon and in a moment it
would be covered. Robin hesitated, hoping for the dark. He
did not want to cross over to the stables in full moonlight.
He steadied his breathing and took advantage of the moment
to fold the top of his pillowcase more securely. It was a difficult sort of bundle and perhaps it had been a mistake to take
the whole beef bone. But there had been no time to cut it
off, and when there was a pause in their travels the puppy
would enjoy playing with it.

He bent to put on his shoes while he waited. Then the
cloud began to move over the bright mirror of the moon and
Robin hurried with the final knot. He hitched up his bundle
and slid away from the wall.

His Aunt Isabella had said that the puppy would be tied up
by the stables, and she was always obeyed to the letter. The
only question was—which stable?

Near him Robin could hear a horse moving restlessly, and
he thought how wonderful it would be to leave by horse-
back, with the spaniel and the bundle safely on the saddle in
front of him. It was, of course, a foolish idea. He had nothing
to feed the horse and they would be seen immediately. Robin
hoped severely that he was not getting lightheaded.

He had been trying to move silently, being careful of his
feet so that they would not rustle in the straw, and it was not
his fault that someone had left a raking fork leaning against
the corner of the wall. It fell with a crash on the cobble-
stones, sounding to Robin's startled ears as if the day of judg-
ment had arrived in one mighty thunderclap. He stood rigid,
waiting for the lights in the house to flare up and for the
stableboys to rush out upon him.

Nothing happened. Perhaps he had overestimated the noise. It was only a rake, after all.

He listened and could hear nothing but frogs. Then he listened again and heard a small whimper.

Robin would have known that sound anywhere and it made him almost weak with relief. At the bottom of his mind he had been afraid that he would never find the little dog at all, but it had been foolish to be frightened. The fall of the rake must have wakened the puppy, and Robin could hear a scrabbling sound as he curled up and tried to go back to sleep again.

Robin knelt and felt cautiously about until his hand closed over a small, cold nose. He held it gently but firmly, and with his other hand he tested the rope with which the puppy had been tied. The knot was too heavy to manage with one hand and so he reached for the penknife in his belt and began to saw the rope through. As he worked he talked to the little dog in a low whisper. He did not want him to feel worried, with his nose being held so tightly, but Robin could not run the risk of letting him bark.

It was hard to cut through the rope with only one hand, and the back of Robin's neck began to prickle with sweat. He kept expecting an accusing hand to fall on his shoulder, and it took all his self-control not to waste time by looking nervously around. He bent his head and sawed at the hempen rope with quick, savage strokes, and all at once the last strand parted.

Robin tucked the puppy under one arm, still holding him so that he could not bark. The puppy settled down confidingly and apparently went to sleep again. He was a very good dog and Robin felt proud of him.

He scooped up his bundle with his free hand and slid along

the shelter of the stable wall. Behind him loomed the great gray bulk of the house, lightless and shut and already somehow a stranger.

A stranger and almost an enemy. If anyone looked out he would be seen, and he broke into a sudden run. All he wanted was to get away from those windows as quickly as he could, and he ran as he had never run before for the sheltering safety of the woods.

Chapter 3

By the time Robin reached the woods a thin rain had started to fall. He was hot from running and excitement, and the damp coolness felt kind against his face. Also it seemed to drop a veil between himself and the world, so that he and the puppy stood safe and alone in the night.

Robin moved cautiously among the trees, careful not to trip over anything, until he was deep in the woods and his eyes had grown accustomed to the darkness. Then he sat down on a fallen log, put his bundle down beside him and drew the puppy gently out from under his arm.

The puppy, with the delightful good sense he had shown all along, did not bark. Instead he threw himself on Robin, licked him devotedly and then settled down to have the rope untied from his neck. It took several minutes, since the knot was wet and Robin's hands were still shaking a little.

He cuddled his dog's head for a moment in his hands and then opened his bundle to get at the beef bone. The pillow-case was not keeping out much of the rain, but it would probably do the cheese good to get wet and nothing ever hurt bread.

With his penknife Robin sawed a piece from the end of the beef bone and cut it into small pieces which he fed the spaniel one by one. No doubt the spaniel would have enjoyed the whole chunk just as much, but Robin could not resist the pleasure of feeding him.

The puppy was hungry but he ate like a gentleman. Robin smoothed his fur and decided that when there was time to give him a good combing there would not be a handsomer spaniel in England. His fingers shaped a curly frill in the wet fur around the dog's neck, and he bent down to whisper to him.

"I shall call you Ruff," he said. "Ruff Wakefield. I love you so."

He then remembered that he had been sent to bed without his supper and sawed off a crust of bread to eat with some of the cheese. But he found he was too excited to swallow and wrapped his bundle up again.

Ruff was beginning to play with his last piece of beef, and Robin decided it was time to leave. He groped about in the wet leaves at his feet until he found a good oak branch. He stripped the leaves from it neatly, pushed one end through his bundle and tied it tightly. Then he tucked Ruff under one arm and straightened, standing still for a moment while he gave himself time to think things out.

The most important thing to do was to make his plans carefully before he started. In the morning a search would be organized, and everyone would be asked about seeing a boy and a spaniel. His chief problem was to keep out of sight and yet at the same time to keep moving. If he could succeed, in the next twenty-four hours, in putting thirty miles or so between himself and his Aunt Isabella, he would have a reasonable chance of success.

Four miles an hour was a good pace, and if he could keep it up he would be a long way by nightfall. But he would have to circle towns and villages, and that would cut down the distance he could put between himself and the house. Also, he would probably have to stop to rest occasionally, and what with one thing and another he would be lucky to make twenty-five miles, as the crow flies, by nightfall.

There was one thing more. Whatever happened he must never permit himself to run, unless it was actually to avoid capture. Anyone will chase a runner, if only out of curiosity, and that was especially true of farmhands and dogs. He had often seen a rabbit break wildly for open country when if it had stayed under cover a few minutes longer it would have been safe.

If anyone saw him, the best thing to do was to slow down to a saunter and look relaxed. If necessary he could recite Latin verbs to himself to occupy his mind. The thing of chief importance was not to get excited or to look frightened. He would pretend to himself that he was a boy named Henry Gosling who lived in the next village, and that his bundle contained dressed chickens that his mother was sending to market.

The other problem was which way to go, and he had better think that out, too, before he started. It would be foolish to travel at random, especially as he could easily end up going about in a circle.

Robin had never seen a map of Suffolk and he did not know exactly where he was in it. But he did know that the sea lay somewhere to the east, and in one of the port towns along the coast there would surely be work for a willing boy. He was small but he was wiry, and he was sure that he could unload fish. The two of them would not eat much, and his clothes would last for a long time. A shilling a week would be enough to live on, and it should not be difficult to earn a shilling.

Once the sun came up he would be certain of his direction.

In the meantime he knew that the little stream at the foot of the woods ran south, and if he crossed it and kept on moving, he could adjust his course at sunrise.

He gave Ruff an encouraging tickle under the chin and settled his stick on his shoulder. So far, things had gone well. All that was needed now was reasonable caution and a good pair of feet.

Before he waded the stream, Robin took off his shoes and stockings. He had to be mindful of the leather and he had no wish to squelch about in wet shoes half the morning. He had waded it often enough, and he knew exactly where to put his feet.

There was a low whistling call down among the reeds and Robin jumped. He stood still, with the water curling about his knees and listened. Then he relaxed and grinned. It was an otter, doing a little night fishing. Robin might turn into a fisherman himself when he reached the coast, and he wished the otter good hunting.

When the eastern sky began to pale and the trees took on the shape of day, Robin found that he was slightly off his course. He had been working a little too much toward the north. He stopped a moment to rest and catch his breath, and now that the sun was up, he set Ruff down on the ground. The spaniel was certainly not going to be carried all the way to the coast, with four fine legs of his own.

Ruff galloped about in a series of narrowing circles, his ears flapping with excitement. Then he barked sharply at the birds, who were beginning to wake up and who promptly talked back at him.

Robin turned and walked away, resisting the impulse to look back over his shoulder, and Ruff gave one final bark at an indignant hedge-sparrow. Then he settled down at his owner's left heel and Robin felt a warm glow of pride. Ruff would make a good, responsible traveler.

It was just as well he could be trusted, for Robin had many things to watch. The world was waking up, and he and his dog were no longer alone in it. The milkmaids would soon be coming out, swinging their pails, and in the thatched cottages the housewives were getting breakfast. The cattle grazing in the marshlands would have cowherds to watch them, and since it was time to sow the wheat the oxen would be plowing the village strips. In the woods there would be swine rooting about for acorns, and even a very sleepy swineherd could report the passing of a boy and a dog.

Robin moved carefully, always listening. If he heard a rooster crow he shifted his direction, and when he saw a church tower gray against the sky he made a wide detour. He had heard somewhere that there were nearly six hundred parishes in Suffolk, each no doubt with its little church, and he hoped that most of them were not huddled together in the eastern part of the county. There would be time enough to meet some villagers when he started looking for work. All he wanted for the present was a clear path and Ruff safe at his heels.

Once or twice as he reached the top of some little hill he could see a road in the distance, winding its smooth and purposeful way through the green fields. On a road like that, a person could make thirty miles a day. But he might also hear a horseman coming up behind him, and then feel a heavy hand on his shoulder. It was better to keep to the woods. It would always be possible to travel at night, if necessary, to make up for lost time.

Robin had no difficulty about the drinking water. They

crossed several little brooks, with Ruff splashing about until
he looked more like a water rat than a respectable spaniel.
Once Robin saw an eel and might have tried to catch it if
there had been any way of building a fire afterward. But he
did not like the idea of eating it raw, and in any case there
was plenty of bread and cheese for his noon dinner. He found
some wild blackberries, fat and juicy, and carried them in his
cap to eat as he went along.

In the middle of the afternoon Robin decided to change
his shoes because his feet were not as happy as they should
be. He found it was nearly impossible to get the other pair
on, although they usually fitted him quite well. Perhaps he
should have brought his shoeing-horn along with him instead
of leaving it to hold down the letter on his bed.

Ruff began to lag, and Robin picked him up and carried
him under one arm. He seemed to have grown heavier, and
Robin suppressed a strong temptation to stop walking himself. All he really wanted to do was to sit down under the
nearest elm, put his head against the gentle trunk and go to
sleep.

Perhaps it had been a mistake to try to do four miles an
hour. If he walked a little more slowly and stopped oftener
to catch his breath, he might very well be able to manage another ten miles before dusk. It would not do to let himself
get overtired. It might make him careless. He would begin
thinking of hot meat pies when he should be thinking only
of carefulness and silence.

Behind him the sun sank lower through the trees. Rooks
began to fly in long strings through the sky, wheeling and
diving with what seemed to Robin an incredible amount of
energy, and some swifts dashed about in the air, shouting like
screech-owls.

Foolishness, thought Robin. They ought to sit down and rest. He himself kept on moving, talking to his feet in a cheerful way so that they would feel encouraged. He was afraid that if he once let himself sit down he would not get up again, and it was not until the last glow had left the west that he finally stopped and set down his burdens. After dark it would be easy to lose his way.

He did not take his shoes off, since he suspected he would not be able to get them on again. But as a special treat he allowed himself a small piece of Ruff's beef, putting it between two slices of bread to make it last longer. Ruff did not want the beef because he had caught a mole that afternoon, and it cheered Robin up immensely.

He then remembered that he had not said his prayers the night before. He always said his prayers before he went to bed, and since he had not gone to bed the matter had escaped his mind entirely. In an effort to adjust the balance he said them twice, while the black leaves rustled gently over his head.

Then he settled his head down on his bundle and found that the end that held his shirts made an excellent pillow. Ruff curled up under his arm, leaving out only his tail to the night winds, and Robin put a protective hand over the soft fur.

Somewhere an owl hooted. It was probably out looking for food for its young, searching along the hedges and then returning to some church tower to feed its children. It was a responsibility, having a young thing in your care. Robin rolled over slightly, to protect his puppy from the chill of the night, and by the time the moon came up they were both asleep.

Chapter 4

Robin overslept. The sun was accusingly high in the sky when he reluctantly opened his eyes, and it glittered down through the leaves with almost the strength of noon. Robin, still fogged with dreams, stared at it for a moment as though he had never seen the sun before in his life.

Ruff was sitting quietly beside him with the alert and virtuous look of one who has been up for hours. Robin caught him up and rolled over in the grass with him, and the puppy gave a yelp of joy at the opportunity to wrestle. Robin, abruptly sobered, let him go again. Someone might hear them, and they were not there to play.

He smoothed down his hair and brushed his jerkin, making himself look as neat as possible. This was the day on which he started to look for work, and he wanted to make as good an impression as possible. When he came to the next village he would inquire how far he was from the sea.

Since Robin was already on the slope of a hill he climbed to the top of it to get the lay of the land. Quite unexpectedly he found himself looking down on a large town, whose walls curved to the side of a river that glittered in the sun. He followed the river with his eyes, one hand shading them from the light, and he could see it widening in the distance until, far away, it reached an open stretch that might be the sea.

No one would notice a boy and a dog in such a busy town,

and it would be an excellent place to make inquiries. Robin straightened his cap carefully, smoothed Ruff's ears and started downhill, even permitting himself a cheerful whistle as he walked along.

It was apparently a market day, and a stream of people were coming in through the low arched gate as Robin slipped into town. He felt almost as safe as in a forest of trees, and the churches and houses pressed so closely that they were almost as good a shelter as the people. He walked slowly, trying to look like an interested shopper, and came to a halt at the Market Cross. This must be the center of town, with all the stalls spread out with meat and apples and butter and cheese and pots and pans. Everyone was shouting and arguing and filling their baskets, and Robin was glad to be in such a fine, lively town.

Near him was a fish stall, and its wares looked so large and flat and unfamiliar that Robin was sure they must have come from the sea. The owner was a little old man with bright blue eyes, equipped with a large apron and a heavy pair of gloves. He was having a difficult time keeping his charges on the boards of the stall. They were large and slippery and he fought with them grimly.

Robin jumped forward just in time to catch a large gray fish that was slipping off backward to the paving stones. He and the owner heaved together wordlessly and it moved back into place.

"Stupid things," said the old man bitterly. "I can't abide fish in any form."

"I'm sorry, sir," said Robin politely. It seemed a little odd, under the circumstances, that he should be selling them.

"Silly, slippery, goggle-eyed things," said the old man, glaring at his unresponsive wares. "Heavy, too. It's my daughter-in-law's booth," he added. "My son is a fisherman."

"Are we near the sea?" asked Robin eagerly.

"Surely," said the old man in mild contempt for such ignorance. "Follow the river a matter of ten miles or so and there you are."

"Could a boy find work there?" asked Robin.

"I doubt it," said the old man candidly. "Everything is licensed, you know. Even a booth like this has to be licensed. And the towns don't like labor coming in from the outside. Masterless men and boys. They try to keep them out. Very careful towns we have around here."

Robin tried to keep his face looking calm and unconcerned. But the old man must have noticed something because his voice became kinder.

"Can you handle a boat?"

"No, sir," said Robin in a low voice.

"I thought I might speak to my son about you when he came home tonight. But if you can't handle a boat—" He sighed. "If I had a penny, lad, I would give it to you, but I hardly see any spending money of my own from one Michaelmas to the next. It is an unkind world. I might add that we have a law here in Ipswich about dogs going around loose. The town says they have to be muzzled. Eightpence fine." He looked benignly at Ruff. "Or maybe it's tenpence."

Robin scooped Ruff up in one frantic movement and tucked him securely inside his jacket. He had a most peculiar feeling of panic, as though he were trapped in a room with no way of escape. But he forced his voice to remain steady. "Thank you, sir."

"What you should do," said the old man instructively, "is to learn a trade. If you apprentice yourself to a good master, you'll be able to set up in business for yourself in no time at all."

"How long would it take?" asked Robin.

"For the apprenticeship," admitted the old man, "seven years. But time passes quickly when you're young." He surveyed his rows of fishes thoughtfully. "Of course there would be papers to be signed. Your father or your guardian would have to make the arrangements. There are all kinds of rules." He sighed again. "I sometimes feel that there are too many rules in England. But that is the way things have always been, and no doubt it is the way they will always be. It keeps things tidy, no doubt." He looked at Robin a little anxiously. "Cheer up, lad."

"Is there anywhere," said Robin carefully, "that a boy could go? A boy like me who needs work?"

"You might try London," said the old man.

"London!" said Robin softly. Meg had visited London

once, and she told him about it sometimes while he was having his supper in the nursery. It had remained in Robin's mind as a city of magic, a place of glittering towers and processions with banners and kings and queens. But of course it was a real city. It must be.

"In a big city like that," said the old man, "people come and go and no one notices them much. You could probably pick up work there, a good, willing lad like you."

"How far is it to London, sir?" asked Robin.

The old man frowned thoughtfully. "Matter of eighty miles or so, I should say. The carters make it in three days, but they always take their time unless they're freighting butter. . . . Take your hands off that fish, lady, unless you're going to buy it."

"How can I tell if it's fresh?" demanded the woman, shifting her basket and preparing for battle.

Robin rubbed his nose and tried to think. Eighty miles would be easy enough if he had something to eat along the way, but walking made a person very hungry. He reckoned up what was left of the bread and cheese and knew he would eat it all in the first twenty miles. And he would not dare to travel through any of the towns and villages in case they all had laws against little dogs.

"And it was fresh caught yesterday!" said the old man, returning from the fray. "What a fine world it would be if there were no people in it. Old hen!"

"Sir," said Robin, "may I ask you one more question?"

"Certainly, lad," said the old man graciously.

Robin fished in his wallet and brought out the coin he had once found on the landing. "Could you tell me what this is worth?"

The old man peered at it with interest. "Foreign," he said. "Looks Dutch. I would say it was a Dutch florin."

Robin rubbed it against the sleeve of his jacket. "It looks like silver."

"Oh, it's silver right enough. But you never know with these foreign coins. We get a lot of them in a port town like this, and the rate of exchange keeps shifting. No one likes them much." He peered at it again. "But it would buy you a good meal at any of the inns in town, and a warm bed."

"Thank you," said Robin. "Which is the nearest inn?"

"Straight ahead," said the old man, pointing with his knife. "Keep St. Mary's Tower behind you, and where the roads cross you'll find plenty of inns. Take your choice and good luck go with you."

"Thank you, sir," said Robin again. He looked down to make sure that Ruff was well hidden and then shouldered his stick. He was sorry he did not have anything to give the old man who had been so kind to him.

"Enjoyed your company," said the old man unexpectedly, and again he said, "Good luck."

It was easy enough to find the inns. It would have been more difficult to avoid them. They were splendid inns with great handsome creaking signs. The problem was to find any carters. They had apparently loaded their carts and left town early in the morning, and it was now almost noon.

It had been such a good idea, too. The florin would have been enough to pay for the ride to London, and even if it took three days no one could get very hungry just sitting on a cart. Whenever they passed a town Robin could have hidden Ruff under one of the boxes and he would have been safe until they reached the end of the journey.

Robin tried four inns, but at each of them the carters had left at dawn. It would be the same everywhere, a stableboy told him, chewing a straw and looking mildly sympathetic.

Robin knew that if he waited until tomorrow his bread and cheese would never last out. He was already beginning to think about his dinner, although he tried not to, and then there would be the problem of supper that evening and the whole day wasted.

"Why not try the blacksmith's?" asked the stableboy, still chewing. "Henry Huggen had a shoe loose on his horse and he may still be in town."

Robin took three wrong turnings before he found the blacksmith's shop. He knew he was trying to move too fast and forced himself to quiet down and think what he was doing. But it was too late in any case. The blacksmith was alone at his forge, singing strongly to himself and very much off key.

"Sir," shouted Robin, "has Mr. Henry Huggen been here today?"

"Yes," said the blacksmith, pausing. "You wanted him?"

"I wanted him very much."

"He's on his way to London," said the blacksmith, "and so he must have left by the west gate. If you hurry you should be able to catch up with him. Go straight up Cornhill, and if you don't see him before you leave town follow the road that turns south over the marshes."

"Thank you very much," said Robin gratefully. "How will I recognize him?"

"The horse is an old bay," said the blacksmith. "Rather heavy shanks and the fetlock joint a little stiff. There's a scar on one pastern, and I put a new shoe this morning on his right front hoof." He paused. "I think old Huggen was wearing a gray coat, although it may have been blue. But you can't miss the horse." He turned back to his forge and his great voice rose cheerily upward with the sparks.

Robin turned and ran. The west gate was evidently the one he had entered that morning. He raced up Cornhill, clutching Ruff tightly to keep him out of sight, and butted his way through the shoppers in a way he knew that no gentleman should. There were plenty of carts, all going the wrong way to be Mr. Huggen's, and Robin dodged among the wheels with no regard for the upraised whips.

When he reached the west gate he was panting, but he did not dare to stop for breath. He skidded to the left and ran down the wide road, the dust leaping up under his heels.

He knew he was too late, and when a long rise of ground curved in front of him he nearly gave up trying. But he doggedly kept on running and when he reached the top he had his reward. Small in the distance was a single cart, slowly moving south.

Chapter 5

Robin was too much out of breath to shout. He ran down the hill in a final burst of speed, hitched Ruff up under one arm and swung himself over the back of the wagon. Then he crawled carefully through the barrels and boxes and arrived panting at the driver's seat. Mr. Huggen was a very fat man so that he took up most of it, and his heavy coat was gray-green.

Robin sat struggling to catch his breath, and Mr. Huggen gave him a look of mild surprise. He had a round face and small sleepy eyes, and he did not look especially friendly.

"Sir," said Robin, "may I ride to London with you?"

"No," said Mr. Huggen. He turned his attention to the horse and slapped the reins thoughtfully. "Get off," he added.

"I can pay," said Robin. He held out the florin, which had been clutched in his fist ever since he had started out on his search of the inns. "It's made of silver."

Mr. Huggen turned his slow, sleepy eyes to the coin. He released one large hand from the reins and held it out, and the coin looked very small and lonely as he stared at it meditatively. He bit it. Then he lapsed into silence.

"Sir?" said Robin hopefully.

"Very well," said Mr. Huggen, and clucked to the horse.

Robin relaxed and was surprised to find how tightly he had been holding himself. He set Ruff down in his lap and began smoothing the top of the dog's head, to give his hands something to do for a moment.

They rode for a mile or so in silence.

"How long will it take to get to London, Mr. Huggen?" Robin asked finally.

"Day after tomorrow," said Mr. Huggen. "You talk a great deal. Do you intend to talk all the time?"

"No, sir," said Robin, and lapsed into silence again.

Day after tomorrow. At that rate, Ruff's beef would certainly last out. The bread and cheese probably would not, unless Robin were very careful, but he could make thin slices with his knife and since he was not walking there was no reason why he should become very hungry. Perhaps the old horse would amble past some berry bushes and Robin could pick himself a few.

He could certainly plan to go without his noon dinner, to get himself into the habit of eating less.

When Mr. Huggen unwrapped a huge meat pasty and buried his face in it, Robin tried to think of other matters. He recited the alphabet to himself backward, since that is a difficult thing to do, and finally he slipped off the cart and found himself a piece of grass to chew.

All afternoon the long green miles rolled behind them, and only once did Mr. Huggen volunteer an unsolicited statement. He had sent Robin to the back of the cart to steady a barrel that had jarred loose, and when Robin returned to report success Mr. Huggen made his statement. "Bad things, barrels," he said.

It was clear that the man could talk under certain circumstances, and Robin tried to encourage him to keep on with the conversation. It was like a game, and it kept Robin's mind off the subject of food.

By the end of the afternoon he had found out that horse-shoes were more expensive than they should be and that Mr. Huggen lived in London. Robin tried to draw him out on this wonderful subject, but all he could discover was that Mr. Huggen lived near Aldgate and that rents were going up. Robin's own vision of the capital city was a confused mixture of the Tower of London, the Queen's palace and the Widow of Watling Street. Mr. Huggen said that the Queen did not live in London, and he then retired into a silence so impenetrable that Robin's questions beat against it in vain.

That night they stopped at an inn in Colchester, and Mr. Huggen went inside to his supper and his warm bed. Robin subdivided his cheese carefully to make it last longer and then spent the evening combing Ruff and talking to him while he fed him bits of beef. He told Ruff all about London and Ruff listened intelligently.

Robin found it hard to get to sleep that night, perhaps because he was so hungry. It was not easy to find a comfortable place among the boxes and barrels and it was rather cold out there in the innyard. He lay staring into the dark side of the cart a long time before he fell asleep.

In the morning a remarkable thing happened. One of the maids at the inn came out and found him, curled up and blinking, among the barrels. She smiled at him and went indoors, and then returned a few minutes later with what looked, incredibly, like a large buttered bun. Inside it were two slices of cold chicken.

"Go on," she said. "Eat it."

She stood with her hands on her hips and watched him while he chewed it slowly and reverently. It was the most wonderful gift he had ever been given. But when he tried to thank her properly, she reached out and ruffled his hair affectionately and then turned and went back into the inn.

Colchester was clearly a remarkable town, with remarkable people in it, and Robin wished they could stay longer. One of the stableboys told him it had been built by King Cole, who lived in a castle on the north side of town and went forth from time to time to do battle with his enemies. Another stableboy said firmly it had been built by one of King Alfred's sons, and someone else claimed it was the Romans who had put up the walls.

Aside from all this valuable information, Robin made the more practical discovery that he was no longer in Suffolk but in Essex. He had never been out of his own county before and he looked about him with interest. But everything seemed to be about the same, and the same green fields and woods stretched on either side of the cart as he and Mr. Huggen rode along.

Assisted by the bun, Robin was able to hold himself successfully to his ration of bread and cheese. The bread was growing a little moldy, probably because it had been rained on, but it was still nutritious. Robin ate his supper very slowly that night to make it last longer.

The beef was holding up well, but the following morning Robin sliced it from the bone and wrapped it carefully, giving the bone to Ruff to play with. Ruff, instantly delighted, took it to the back of the cart and worried it all morning. He mislaid it twice and Robin searched for it anxiously among the barrels, since Mr. Huggen would not want to find a stray bone in his possession after he reached London.

According to what Mr. Huggen had said, today was the day they would arrive. Robin tried to sit quietly, but a kind of shiver ran up his spine and his eyes kept searching the road in front of him for some sign of castles and towers. It was good grazing country, better than his own Suffolk, but Robin had seen a cow before and he kept his eyes fixed on the horizon. The traffic on the road was growing heavy, which was surely a good sign.

Toward the middle of the afternoon Robin gave a jump. He was sure he had seen something to the southwest that was neither a farmhouse nor a cloud. He waited a few minutes until he was certain and then he laid a hand on Mr. Huggen's sleeve. It was true that Mr. Huggen did not actually go to sleep while he drove, but on the other hand it took a good deal to attract his attention.

As soon as Mr. Huggen's eyes were on him, Robin pointed excitedly but wordlessly to the horizon. Mr. Huggen's ways were catching and Robin had almost lost the art of conversation.

"St. Paul's Cathedral," said Mr. Huggen, and a look almost

of satisfaction passed over his round face. "We made good time."

There was a pause. "It is on a hill, you know," Mr. Huggen added unexpectedly. "You can see the whole city from there."

Robin leaned forward with his mouth open. But nothing much happened and St. Paul's disappeared behind a grove of trees. There were some windmills in the nearer distance, and then the houses began to thicken. They became almost continuous, with their little garden plots and their chickens, and to the right of the road were two big round wooden buildings with thatched roofs.

"What are those, Mr. Huggen?" Robin asked. "What are those?"

Mr. Huggen did not answer. He was watching the road, now that the traffic had become more complicated. He kept his hands on the reins and clucked to the bay horse encouragingly.

Robin could see ahead of him what must be London Wall, with an arched gate set into it, and he stood up in the cart in his excitement. Mr. Huggen reached out a large hand and pulled him down again.

"Might fall," he said in explanation. "Keep calm, boy," he added.

They went in under the arched gate and Robin told himself that he was in London. But the town looked very much like Colchester, except that of course there were more people. Wherever Robin looked he could see little parish churches, with their narrow spires pricking into the sky, and the streets were crowded with houses and shops that pressed close to the road. But there was no river Thames to be seen, and no castles.

They passed a few inns but Mr. Huggen did not stop. Then they reached a wide street and Robin was convinced they would never get across, with so many other carts and horses fighting their way with the same determined fury that Mr. Huggen was suddenly showing. Then, all at once, they had crossed it triumphantly and Mr. Huggen turned into an inn-yard on his right. The great sign over the door showed a pair of crossed keys against a background of red and yellow.

Robin got down over the wheel, a little stiff after all that sitting, and tucked Ruff carefully under one arm. He shouldered his bundle and held out his hand to Mr. Huggen. "Good-by, sir, and thank you very much."

Mr. Huggen looked down at him. "For what?"

"For the ride, sir."

"You paid for it," said Mr. Huggen. "Why waste breath?" He turned away to look for an ostler to take his horse, and then he glanced back over his shoulder at Robin. "What do you plan to do now, you and the dog?"

That was an easy question to answer. "We are going to the top of St. Paul's, sir, to see the city."

"They charge, you know," said Mr. Huggen with a kind of gloomy satisfaction. "They charge a penny to let you go up."

This had never occurred to Robin, and once more he had the curious feeling of being trapped. But it was foolish to feel like that. There must be other ways of seeing the city.

Mr. Huggen stared at him thoughtfully and then he gave a deep sigh that seemed to come from the soles of his square-toed shoes. He began to mutter to himself and his hand fumbled in his wallet. There was a reluctant clink of coins and he drew out a penny.

"Here, boy," he said. "Take it."

Robin started to protest, since nothing was owed him, but Mr. Huggen pushed the penny into his hand. The ostler came up just then, and the two men embarked on a discussion of the price of oats. Robin said his final "Thank you" to empty air, since no one was paying any attention to him, and then he turned and left the innyard with a light heart. He had a penny and he was going to see all London.

He worked his way back to the intersection and asked directions of the only man who seemed to be standing still in the hurrying crowds. "Straight left," the man said. "Follow Cornhill to Cheapside, and you'll have no trouble in finding St. Paul's."

The houses became taller and more beautiful as Robin walked along. Some of them rose three and four stories high, and Robin could see that London was not just a larger Colchester. When he reached Cheapside and saw the great shopping avenue spread out in front of him, he felt quite awed by its size and its splendor. One row of fourteen shops on the south side of the street rose four stories high and was carved and gilded like some great palace. Robin stopped to stare at the woodmen riding monstrous painted beasts, made apparently of lead and gaily colored, that looked down in splendor at the shoppers below. There was also a great water conduit, most nobly carved, and Robin stopped for a drink to show that he was now a resident of London and knew his way around.

He did not like to admit to himself or to Ruff that he was feeling a little shy, but he could not help catching his breath sharply when the great bulk of St. Paul's Cathedral loomed in front of him. A steady stream of people went in and out, laughing and talking and arguing, and it seemed to Robin that the Londoners must be a very energetic race. He slipped inside and stared up in a hushed silence at the great arches that soared over his head. They had a kind of ancient stillness that took no notice of the chattering, silk-clad citizens who milled about the base of the holy stone. There was an organ somewhere, but it could hardly be heard over the noise of the talking.

Robin paid his penny and with a tight grip on Ruff he turned up the crooked, dark little stairway that led to the roof. He began counting the steps as he went up, and by the time he had reached two hundred and fifty it seemed to him that he must be climbing to the rim of the world. His breath came short, although perhaps it was only with excitement. He went on counting, and just as he reached three hundred there was daylight again and birds flying overhead.

Robin found himself on a flat open roof covered with lead. Various people were strolling about on it, and he decided there was nowhere in London there were not people. Some of them were leaning over the rails, looking down, and Robin went over to join them. He held his cap against the wind, which was rather lively up there.

Robin looked down over the edge and forgot both his cap and the people. He even forgot the hunger that had stalked him all day. He stared down with his mouth open in sheer delight, for beneath him was the whole of London. It lay like a tapestry, like a jewel, like a toy city, gleaming in the late afternoon light with the river cutting through it like a ribbon of silk. It was the true city of his dreams, and Robin drew a deep breath and stood still in enchantment.

Chapter 6

"Be careful there, boy," said a voice behind him. "Those rails have been up a long time and they're a little rotten. You don't want to go down faster than you came up."

Robin pulled his gaze reluctantly away from London and turned to look at an elderly man in black who was smiling at him.

"Yes, it's a fine town," the man said. "I remember how I felt the first time I saw it." He came to stand beside Robin and they both turned back to look at the city.

"Is that the Thames, sir?" asked Robin. "That river?" It was crowded with boats, little ones that looked like water beetles and larger ships whose masts were as thin as twigs from that distance and whose riggings were a filament of cobwebs. Across the river swung a great bridge, heavy with houses and alive with little carts.

"The Thames indeed," said the man with satisfaction. "The finest river in England and probably in the world. I wish I could give you the exact figures on the tonnage the port handles. It would impress you."

Robin was impressed enough already. He leaned out to look more closely, and his new friend put a warning hand on his shoulder.

"You can see just as well from a little farther back," he said. "You will notice the gate just below us. That is Ludgate, and the wide street beyond it leads to Westminster."

"Where the Queen is?" asked Robin.

"Where the Queen is, God bless her. Now turn completely around and look in the other direction, where you see that big white building close to the river. That is the Tower of London, built by William the Conqueror."

Robin had known all along that it would be there, and he stared in delighted satisfaction at the great white battlements. North of the Tower the walls of the city curved around in a huge semicircle that reached back to the river again, and Robin could see each of the seven gates with tiny carts and miniature horses going in and out.

It was easy enough to find the gate through which he and Mr. Huggen had entered. It lay northwest of the Tower, and beyond it were the windmills and the two round wooden buildings with the thatched roofs. Looking down at them both from his lofty eminence, Robin could see they were hollow inside and open to the sky. He pointed them out to his new friend, who gave a small cluck of disapproval.

"Those," he said reluctantly, "are theatres. A good boy like you would not wish to know about such things."

Robin was not sure he was as good a boy as all that. "What is wrong with them?" he asked with interest.

"They are sinks of iniquity," said the man firmly. "Dens of sin. The players strut about on a painted stage and utter wicked words, and they lure in the heedless populace. The city is full of healthsome resorts and it is not at all necessary to go to plays."

"Did you ever go to one?" asked Robin.

"Certainly not," said the man shortly. "You will notice," he added, "that both the theatres you are looking at so intently are built well outside the city walls. The mayor and aldermen are wise and good men, and they would not give

licenses to have such evil things erected within the city of
London. So those wicked men went out to Shoreditch, which
is not under the city government, and there they flaunt their
silks and their playing flags. The same thing is true on the
other side of the river, along the Bankside. The mayor has
no power there either, and it is the haunt of actors and thieves
and vagrants."

Vagrants. Masterless men. A boy who had not yet found
work was a vagrant, and perhaps the laws of London were
just as strict as the laws of Ipswich. Robin held Ruff a little
tighter, and he thought of Shoreditch and the Bankside not
as a den of thieves but as a refuge.

"Is it difficult to find work in London, sir?"

The man drew back, slightly but unmistakably.

"A virtuous and industrious youth," he said, folding his
hands together, "can always find work."

"If you were a virtuous youth," said Robin, "how would
you go about it?"

"I trust you are not being impertinent," said the man.
"There is nothing more unattractive in the young. One becomes apprenticed, of course, just as I did. It is the only
way."

"There is no other, sir?"

"You might advertise. If you leave St. Paul's by the west
door you will notice the handbills posted up on it. You are
quite at liberty to add one of your own to the collection."
He tapped his fingers meditatively on the railing. "May you
have good fortune," he said, and left.

Robin stared after him and then back at the city, lying
gentle and golden in the long rays of the setting sun. The man
had been very kind and he would find work soon. A city as
beautiful as London would surely be welcoming.

Robin reflected with pride that at least he was here, and to prove it he got out his penknife and carved his initials deeply into the leads. The whole surface of the roof was decorated with similar initials, and R W looked very well among them. Robin added a final flourish to the tail of the W, put away his knife and turned to go back down the ancient, winding stairs.

He found the west door without any trouble, and as the man said it was covered with the advertisments that had been fastened up on it. There were offers to teach French in six easy lessons at a shilling apiece, to teach swimming, to carry letters and to train master fencers. There were also workmen's offers, especially gardeners, with a space left at the bottom for the names and addresses of possible employers. But very few of the spaces were filled in. It was apparently not easy to get work in London, even if you knew all the very best ways to trim apple trees.

Robin left the Cathedral and stood at the top of the hill outside, thinking hard. He could not just drift around the city, hoping that something would turn up. It was a very big city, busy and full of people, and he could not expect anyone to care what happened to him.

Enough scraps were left of the bread and cheese to give him a final supper for tonight, and Ruff's beef would last through tomorrow. He reckoned up his other available assets. Safe in his wallet was his father's signet ring, which of course he could not sell. But he had three shirts in the bundle and one of them was linen. It ought to be possible to get a fairly good price for a linen shirt, if he could find a district where there was a dealer in secondhand clothes. With the money from that, he and Ruff could be sure of food for a week or more. On the other hand, he would have to be care-

ful how he went about selling the shirt. He did not want to
be accused of stealing it.

Robin decided to give himself one more day. He had a use
for the shirts himself, with winter coming on, and perhaps by
this time tomorrow he would have found work. He had done
quite well so far, and perhaps his luck would hold.

He slept that night under a bookstall in St. Paul's Church-
yard. It was a quiet place after dark, with no risk of being
stepped on, and the planks had been solidly built to support
the weight of the books above them.

Ruff was a little restless during the night and Robin decided it was because he had not had any chance to run about.
He promised his dog that as soon as the sun came up he
would take him into the fields north of the city and give him
a chance to stretch his legs. It grew cold in the night and
Robin got out two of his shirts and tucked them about Ruff,
smoothing him gently behind the ears until the spaniel finally
fell asleep.

London woke early and became noisy as soon as it was
awake. Large, fat, well-fed apprentices set out their masters'
wares, whistling cheerfully in the pale morning light, and
coal sellers, pie sellers, water sellers and apple sellers all began shouting at the top of their voices as they moved
through the streets. Carts clattered over the paved roads,
householders leaned out of upstairs windows and shouted to
their friends across the way, and the sun rose high and strong
with a special London brightness.

It was a fine autumn day, and Robin felt sure that any boy
could expect good luck in such weather. He had also made
the useful discovery that tightening his belt an extra notch
made him feel a little less hungry.

Robin thought he had the whole map of the city clearly in

his head, but he found that things were more complicated at ground level. Twice he lost himself in a narrow tangle of alleys and ended up at the river, and even when he was most careful to ask directions he found that the streets had a way of taking a slight twist and losing themselves and him. This was especially true of the residential district north of Cheapside, and Robin encountered the same parish church three times before he finally corrected his direction.

He was looking for Moorgate, which led directly into the north fields. It was only fair to give Ruff a chance to stretch his legs, and Robin did not dare to put him down in the crowded city streets. But the gate was small and hard to find, and it was nearly noon before he slipped through it triumphantly and saw the familiar windmills in the distance.

Robin set Ruff down in the tall yellowing grass and the spaniel leaped about with his ears flapping. It occurred to Robin that he might be able to find a few mushrooms and he looked for them in a vague kind of way while Ruff circled about him. The tightened belt had not been quite as much help as he had hoped, and after a while he sat down in the grass. Nothing was the matter with him except that he felt a little tired. He had not had any breakfast, and he had been walking all morning.

Ruff leaped into his arms, intent on play, and Robin wrestled with him gently. He hoped he was not prejudiced, but it seemed to him that Ruff was looking very beautiful. On the trip south Robin had spent most of his time combing Ruff's coat so that it gleamed like satin. He was a dog to be proud of. The most beautiful dog, perhaps, in the world.

Robin's head was bent down over the spaniel and he did not see the man in front of him until he was so close that his short, noonday shadow fell over them both. Then Robin looked up, and the man seemed enormous.

He was standing with his legs apart and his hands on his hips. He wore a pair of sea boots, his jerkin was ragged and his black hair fell about his face. Thrust into his leather belt was a heavy knife with a naked blade.

Robin stared at him, one hand thrown protectively across Ruff and the other still lying in the grass. The man leaned his head forward.

"Where did you get that dog?" he said. He had a low, heavy voice, a little thick, and it was hard to make out what he was saying.

"He's my dog," said Robin, and he was ashamed that his voice shook a little.

"He's my dog now," the man said.

Chapter 7

Robin's throat was so dry that he could not swallow, and his heart pounded so fast that he could not think. He had never known panic before in his life, and he clutched Ruff so tightly that the dog stirred unhappily under his hand.

"Give him to me," said the man, leaning forward.

Robin forced the panic back with what was almost a physical effort. He was not going to help Ruff by getting frightened, like a baby.

He stole a quick glance around the field. There were people walking about, mostly in family groups of two and three, but they were too far away to be any help. Also the man had a knife, and a knife can be used very quickly and silently.

If only he were not in such a bad position on the grass! But he was sitting with both feet sprawled out in front of him.

"Sir," said Robin, "please don't take my dog away from me."

The man laughed.

"Please, sir, please," said Robin, getting up on one knee in supplication.

The man laughed again. Apparently he liked the feeling of having someone kneel on the ground in front of him.

Robin dug the toe of his right foot firmly into the grass and steadied his knee. Then he flung himself directly forward, hunching his shoulders around Ruff to protect him from the impact and diving with all his force at the man's legs.

His position had been exactly right, like a runner crouched for a race, and the thief, caught by surprise, was thrown off balance. He went over backward and down into the grass. It was a most satisfying moment.

Robin scrambled to his feet, not daring to stop for his bundle. He tucked Ruff under one arm and raced across the grass without a backward look. He had seen a brick wall and there must be a door in it somewhere.

Most of the people who had been walking in the fields were going in the same direction, and as Robin drew nearer he could see that a well-worn path led to an opening in the wall. People meant safety, and Robin slipped in among them gratefully, loosening his hold slightly on Ruff. He had been clutching him so tightly that the dog had begun to whimper.

Once Robin looked behind him, and his hold on Ruff tightened again. The thief was following them. He looked as big as ever, and the only difference was that his face was black with anger. But he kept to the edge of the crowd and did not try to push his way forward.

Robin slipped in front of a girl who was wearing a very wide farthingale. Her skirt stretched out stiffly and fashionably on both sides of her and would make a kind of screen for the moment at least.

He went on moving, keeping always in front of the girl, and suddenly realized where he was. The big round building in front of him was a theatre, one of those he had passed yesterday with Mr. Huggen and then seen again from the top of St. Paul's. There was a flag flying from the top of the thatched roof, and the people around him were forming in line to see the play.

Robin stood in line, too, grateful for the company. Latecomers lined up behind him, and the girl in the farthingale gave him a quick smile as they moved forward. She was a pleasant-looking girl and Robin smiled back at her with a whole heart. He liked her because her skirt was so wide.

"That is a pretty little dog you have there. What is his name?"

"Ruff, madam," said Robin, and he gave her the low bow he had been taught to give a lady. This was rather difficult to do, since the line had become tightly wedged. They had almost reached the door of the theatre and a man was standing there holding out a box.

"Penny apiece," said the man, shaking the box so that the coins inside it clinked. "One and all, a penny apiece. Hurry up there, boy! You're blocking the whole line."

Robin stared at him in dismay. It had not occurred to him that he would need money to get inside the theatre. All he had thought of was the necessity to escape the huge man lurking at the edge of the crowd.

He had no money, and nothing to offer. He thought longingly of his bundle, lying somewhere in the trampled grass with all his possessions inside of it. But even if he had it now, it was not likely that the man would be willing to accept a linen shirt or a comb to stuff inside his little box.

He turned a stricken face and the girl behind him caught his eye. "He is with me," she said. "I am paying for both."

She had a soft voice, surely the most beautiful in the world.

Once inside the theatre Robin tried to thank her properly but the girl only laughed. She had a pretty laugh, too.

"It happens to everyone," she said. "And I liked your bow."

The penny was apparently for general admission. The girl

was planning to meet her escort inside at one of the expensive upstairs seats in the galleries. But she told Robin that he would be able to see the whole play if he stood inside the theatre in the stage yard and looked up at the raised platform where the players would do the show. Then she smiled again and left him, and Robin hoped that her fortunate escort was an earl at the very least.

He lingered by the door as the theatregoers kept on streaming in. It was not likely that the thief had a penny or would be willing to spend it to get inside the theatre if he had, but Robin wanted to make quite sure. He stood there for nearly half an hour and then decided he was safe. There was evidently no other entrance to the stage yard, since it was easier to control the customers if they all came in by the same door.

Robin gave a huge sigh of relief and realized how tensely he had been holding himself. He relaxed, rubbed his arms and looked about him.

He was in a theatre, that den of iniquity, and it looked wonderful. Around three sides the galleries were filling with people as gay as flowers, laughing and talking and occasionally smacking their children, and in front of him in the flat open space of the yard the rest of the audience was packing itself in as tightly as mice in a nest, standing and waiting for the show to begin. Robin decided that if he wanted to see the play he had better find himself a place in the yard before all the room was taken.

He moved forward and found himself a very good place next to a stout man in a blue wool cap. If Robin were going to be wedged, he might as well find something soft to be wedged against, and the man was as comfortable as a cushion. Robin moved Ruff up to his shoulder so that he would be able to see everything that was going on, and then he waited expectantly for the play to begin.

The bare, uncurtained stage jutted out about level with Robin's head, with two great pillars to support its sloping roof. At the back was a painted curtain, with what seemed to be a hunting scene on it full of horsemen and dogs. Above were balconies, curving around the stage and also curtained, and arching over the stage was a painted sky with the signs of the zodiac gleaming in blue and gold. There was gold everywhere, in fact, and the carved woodwork glittered with red and blue paint and much gilding.

Somewhere overhead a trumpet sounded, three strong blasts that made Robin jump and sent a quiver down his back. He fixed his eyes anxiously on the stage doors, since no one knew what might come out from behind them. A dragon perhaps, or a knight in armor. The fat man next to him began to eat nuts, cracking the shells strongly with his teeth, and Robin longed to tell him to be quiet.

There was a fanfare of trumpets that drowned out even the nuts, and then the shrill, reedy music of hautboys. The doors on each side of the stage opened, and from one side came a king, ruffed and sceptered and crowned, with a throng of noblemen in magnificent clothes marching behind him. From the other side came a queen, moving in the same stately manner and led by the hand of a tall man in crimson velvet and silver lace. He was a very handsome man, and Robin looked at him admiringly. A group of noblemen followed the queen also, and the boards of the stage shook beneath such a combination of dignity and splendor.

The tall man in crimson knelt before the king and was created the first Duke of Suffolk. Robin was charmed by the honor that was being shown his home county and could not help developing a proprietary interest in the handsome duke. When the queen said he was loved by all the ladies of France, Robin could see that this might well be so, and he watched with excited interest whenever the Duke of Suffolk came onstage. This was history apparently, the past history of England, and Robin told himself that he could hardly be said to be wasting his time. It was all highly educational.

The queen did not have very good manners. She dropped her fan, and when the Duchess of Gloucester refused to pick it up, the queen gave her a box on the ear. Some of the people around Robin started to laugh as soon as this scene began, so they must have seen the play before. Robin did not laugh, although he wanted to. He had been brought up to be respectful to ladies and he did not want to hurt the Duchess of Gloucester's feelings.

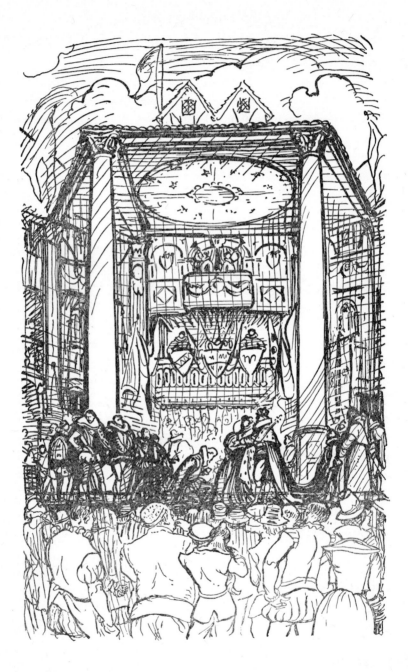

The duchess, however, was a rather wicked woman. There was a scene in her garden, with trees rising up from nowhere as far as Robin could see, and she emerged on her balcony to watch an evil spirit being conjured up below. It was night, as Robin could tell by the dialogue,

> The time of night when Troy was set on fire,
> The time when screech-owls cry . . .

A witch did some mysterious things, thunder crashed overhead, and there was terrible lightning. Robin held Ruff tightly, in case he should feel alarmed, and suddenly there was a tremendous explosion of smoke and flame. Something like a great black bat rose up on the stage and it was the fiend himself.

Robin tried to keep calm, telling himself it was only a play, but he had never been so excited in his life. He looked around at the fat man, to see how he was taking it, but the fat man was still chewing nuts, staring ahead with a bland and unmoved face. He had also found himself a bottle of ale from somewhere and paused from time to time to take another swallow. It seemed incredible to Robin that anyone could be so unfeeling.

The story went on. It was about a weak king named Henry who was surrounded by wicked noblemen. It turned out, unfortunately, that the Duke of Suffolk was among the wicked ones, but he was certainly a handsome man and there were probably extenuating circumstances.

There was also a very funny duel between a boy named Peter and a man named Horner, fought with sandbags tied to the end of sticks. Robin was wholeheartedly on Peter's side, because Peter was a young apprentice and not used to fight-

ing. Peter was quite sure he was going to be killed and he
made a kind of will in which he left all his possessions to his
friends. The apprentice who got his apron was named Robin,
which was an extraordinary coincidence surely. Then there
was a blast of trumpets and Peter fought splendidly, swinging
his sandbag all over the stage until he finally killed his ad-
versary. The man died rather suddenly, perhaps, but this was
a sudden play.

There were more trumpets, and speeches, and a bed
brought in from somewhere, and at one point what seemed
to be a whole parliament in session. Many members of the
cast had become very angry with the Duke of Suffolk, and
Robin began to worry seriously about his welfare. He seemed
very sure of himself, but Robin was afraid he would come to
a bad end.

Robin's worst fears were suddenly confirmed. The stage
changed to a scene by the seashore, and a group of sailors entered with their prisoners. Among them was the Duke of Suffolk with his hands tied. He was dressed in rags instead of his
usual velvets, but Robin would have recognized that gay,
erect head anywhere.

The sailors threatened to kill him and the duke defied them
all in what seemed to Robin a very stirring speech.

> Great men oft die by vile bezonians.
> A Roman sworder and banditto slave
> Murdered sweet Tully; Brutus' bastard hand
> Stabbed Julius Caesar; savage islanders
> Pompey the Great; and Suffolk dies by pirates.

He was dragged away and Robin was glad that at least he
would be killed offstage. He got the shock of his life when
one of the murderers came back dragging Suffolk's body be-

hind him with one hand. In his other hand, to Robin's complete horror, was the duke's head.

Robin turned frantically for help to the fat man beside him. The man had at last finished his nuts and was searching around in his teeth for any bits that might have escaped him. His face was as placid as ever.

The rest of the audience seemed to be enjoying itself and no one had cried, "Help, murder!" It was probably some kind of a stage trick. Of course it could not be a real head that the man was carrying. But Robin turned his face away from what looked like real blood, and he was greatly relieved when a friend of the duke's hauled the body offstage.

But it was impossible to get rid of that head, and the next time the queen appeared she was bent over it in mourning. By that time, however, Robin had developed a new object for his affections, a man named Jack Cade. He was a bad man also, but extremely brave and resourceful. He had been born under a hedge, which struck Robin as a difficult way to start life, and he would never have been captured by his enemies if he had not been so hungry. Robin's heart went out to him, which put his emotions on the wrong side during most of the fighting. But the fighting itself was splendid, with men in armor rushing about in all directions and brandishing swords, with flags flying and trumpets filling the whole theatre with their din.

Then, suddenly, it was all over. King Henry was still alive but there had been beheadings all over the place. Lord Say's head had been chopped off, along with that of his son-in-law, and brought onstage, and so, unfortunately, had Jack Cade's. By this time, however, Robin had stopped worrying. He was almost sure that the heads were faked, cleverly carved and painted in some way to look real, although he was still a little worried about the blood. Still, the audience seemed happy enough as they began to file out through the single door, still chattering.

Robin drew a deep, contented sigh. It had all been very wonderful. Since it was probably the last play he would ever see, it was fortunate that it had been so full of action, like a whole series of ballad woodcuts brought magically to life.

Now he would have to start thinking about the future again and would have to admit to himself how hungry he was.

He decided to go back to the fields and search for his bundle. He knew in a general way where he had left it and there was still an hour or two of daylight left. The sun had not yet started to drop behind the curve of the theatre's thatched roof.

Robin stood patiently in line waiting his turn to get out the door of the theatre. He was in no hurry, but there was a certain amount of pushing and shoving from people anxious to get home to their suppers. He held back to let a mother with a small baby in her arms go ahead of him, and it was just as well he did. Over its little cap he could see through the door into the crowd outside.

It was also fortunate that the thief was so tall. He was leaning against a post while he waited for Robin, and he was whiling away the time by picking his teeth with the sharp point of his knife.

Chapter 8

Robin turned wildly and tried to push his way back into the theatre and safety. But the people behind him were in a hurry and he could make no headway against that moving wall.

He thought of making a run for it and trying to escape to the fields. But the thief had long legs and it was safer to stay with the crowd.

But the crowd would dissolve. It was already thinning and when everyone had gone home he would be left alone to face the man with the knife. Shoreditch was the place where the vagrants gathered, as the man in St. Paul's had said, and who would care what happened to a boy and his dog?

Suddenly he felt desperately tired. All he wanted to do was to lie down in the trampled grass and go to sleep. He had tried to think and plan and be careful, and none of it had done any good.

Robin knew two oaths, both quite good ones, and he said them to himself fiercely under his breath. He was not angry with the thief but with himself, because he was behaving like such a coward. The Duke of Suffolk would never have given up so easily, or Jake Cade either. Even Peter the apprentice had picked up his sandbag and done the best he could, and Peter did not have a dog like Ruff depending on him.

All that was needed was a minute or so to think things out. The thief would not attack until the crowd had disappeared, and if Robin stood still for a moment nothing was likely to happen.

He leaned back against the timber and plaster wall of the theatre. Then he picked up a blade of grass and began to chew it in a carefully casual kind of way.

It was obvious that he could not get back into the theatre by the door he had just left. Even after the crowd had come out, the thief would see Robin go back and follow him in. But there might be another entrance somewhere, perhaps a small door that the actors used.

Robin, still slowly chewing his piece of grass, began to stroll around the side of the building. He looked about him with a tourist's interest, stopping once to select a new and better piece of grass. He did not hurry, and he forced himself not to look behind him.

If such a door existed, it stood to reason that it must be near the stage area and therefore on the opposite side of the building.

Robin sauntered along in a slow, aimless manner until he estimated that he was nearly halfway around. Then he broke into a sudden run, keeping as close as a shadow to the timbered wall. If the door existed, he ought to have just enough time to get inside before the thief turned the corner.

The door was there, and Robin drew a sob of relief. Four horses were tethered outside by the steps and Robin dived under the nearest one with a murmured apology for not having time to go around. Then he took the steps in two leaps, pushed open the door and found himself safe inside the theatre.

He could see nothing for a moment as he stood against the inside wall, breathing hard. But he could hear talking and laughing coming from somewhere, and the creak of heavy equipment being moved about. Then he was able to make out, just next to him, the dim shape of a staircase, and he turned and slid softly up the stairs. He kept one hand on the rail, moving as carefully as he could, and since the stairs were solidly built they did not creak.

Robin could hear the sound of voices as he reached the top of the stairs and he flattened himself against the wall. His eyes were becoming accustomed to the dim light and he decided that this level of the theatre must hold the dressing rooms. Not far from him a man was muttering to himself as he tried to pull a shirt over his head. The shirt was too tight and Robin heard a rather impressive oath that he would be able to add to his small collection. He felt very grateful to the tight shirt, because it was keeping the man's head safely covered, and he felt equally grateful to the wide staircase that was still leading upward.

The third level was blessedly empty. It was lit only by two small, high windows that caught the light of the westering sun, and Robin moved with great care so as not to crash into anything and set it rolling.

He seemed to be in some kind of a storeroom, and the walls were stacked with what must be the furnishings of former plays, dusty but neat. In one corner was a small armory, with swords and muskets tidily propped against each other, and next to it were two upright coffins. There was a chariot, a pile of gilt crowns, a painted rock, three trees with stuffed apples hanging from them, a bearskin, two large tombs, a cage that looked big enough for a lion, a treble viol with two strings broken, a throne and what appeared to be a small dragon. The dragon had glass eyes and stared at Robin thoughtfully but without malice.

It was a curious sort of place and Robin stepped cautiously, resisting an impulse to look inside the heavy chests that lined the wall. They probably all held costumes, although Robin could not help wondering if one of them harbored the fiend he had seen in the duchess's garden. He turned his face resolutely away, and then he saw the bed.

It stood in the far corner of the room, a huge bed whose canopy was decorated with royal emblems. The coverlet was stiff with embroidery and there were gold tassels all around the edge.

Robin walked over and looked at it longingly. He had been sleeping in some rather cramped places for the last few nights, and he tried to imagine how it would feel to stretch out full length with no one likely to step on him.

It was obviously not safe to leave the theatre until it grew dark. And surely it would do no harm to the bed if he were to lie on it for an hour or so.

He turned the coverlet back carefully, with special regard for the gold tassels, and then sneezed at the dust that he had disturbed. The bed had a dry, musty smell, as though no one had used it for a long time, and the mattress was apparently stuffed with hay. Robin told himself he must be careful not to sneeze again or someone might hear him.

He set Ruff down on a hollow in the middle, and Ruff circled for a moment and then curled up in a comfortable ball. He was a wonderful dog, agreeable to anything and never complaining.

Robin took off his shoes and laid them neatly at the foot of the bed. Then he climbed in, lay down beside Ruff and waited to go to sleep. It did not really matter at what hour of the night he left the theatre, and he might as well sleep for a little time while he had the chance.

But sleep would not come. The hay in the mattress rustled

but the rest of the room was too quiet. The heavy chests were lined up against the wall, and who knew what might be inside them?

If he could not sleep, perhaps he should plan. But when he tried to do any planning, all he could think of was his lost bundle, trampled somewhere in the fields outside the theatre. He had hoped to sell one of the shirts for food, to get meat for Ruff and bread for himself. The way he was feeling now, he did not believe he could do a full day's work even if he could find someone to hire him. Perhaps there was some employer in London who would be willing to feed him first and let him start work afterward.

His mind slipped away to all the mock kings and queens who must have died in this bed, pale in their white night shifts and with painted crowns firmly on their heads. He had seen a cardinal die that afternoon on a smaller bed, shrieking of poison, and he tried to pull his mind away from the vividness of the memory. He decided to think about the handsome Duke of Suffolk instead, but all he could remember about him was a bloody head dangling from his murderer's hand.

Robin told himself to stop thinking about the play. His eyes began to move unhappily around the darkening room and he wondered what had once been locked up in the cage. He hoped it had not been a man. Near it were the two coffins, still upright, and as he stared at them through the shadows it seemed to him that one of them was starting to move.

Robin rolled over, the straw rustling under him, and buried his face in Ruff's fur. He would not think of anything except how much they loved each other. The spaniel half wakened and buried his nose in Robin's neck, and Robin clung to him.

He remembered a song his nurse Meg had once taught him,

something about a man and a maid and a cuckoo. He was not sure of the words but he remembered the tune. It brought back the safe firelit walls of the nursery and his nurse's comfortable shape in her white apron, white as the milk she brought him to drink. Robin hummed it softly to himself while the shadows thickened. The two small squares of window gradually darkened and at last it was night.

It was not quite dark in the room, however. There was a faint light coming through the doorway, and Robin decided it must be the shine of a lantern from the floor below. But the light grew steadily brighter, and then there were voices.

Robin sat up to listen and then hurriedly lay back in the straw, making himself as flat as he could and trying not to breathe.

Two men were coming up the stairs, bringing the lantern with them. Robin could hear a rather heavy older voice saying something and a younger one replying. Robin hoped they were having an interesting conversation. If they were, perhaps they would not notice anything out of the ordinary about the bed in the far corner of the room.

It was the older man who was carrying the lantern. He hung it on a hook over the muskets, his face upturned to the swinging light, and Robin could see his square shoulders and blunt head, with the curly hair just beginning to go a little gray.

The younger man leaned back against one of the coffins and picked up a gilded spear that he began twirling in his long fingers. He was perhaps thirty, with bright hazel eyes and hair the color of a fox's fur. He did not look in the least like the king Robin had seen in the play, for the king had been blond and timid and stooped a little as he walked, but all the same there was a curious kind of resemblance. As for the older man, Robin recognized him at once. He had been the good Duke Humphrey who had been murdered offstage, and Robin was glad to see he was alive again. Both actors were in their street clothes, and the younger one wore a ruff.

"It is not that I object to the extra expense," the older man was saying, "but the same thing happens every time. It is always the next script that is going to justify everything." He sighed. "I am very fond of Dick. I am very fond of the whole Burbage family. But I never knew a group of people with such a well-developed gift for spending money." He sighed again. "That is no reflection on the script, you understand. But I dislike the idea of spending any more money on new properties when the costumes have to be considered, too. How many do you think will be in the cast?"

The younger man put down the spear and was absorbed for a moment in inward mathematics. He used up the fingers of both hands and then apparently lost count. "How big was the cast this afternoon, John?"

"Too big," said the older man.

"Ah," said the younger actor thoughtfully. "Then this one will be too big also."

The older man passed his hand wearily through his hair. "We still have that last bill on the costuming, you know. I was looking at it just this morning. And will you tell me why Dick Burbage wants to invest in another bed when we have two already?"

"There are some who feel that the bed downstairs should be buried with military honors. The hind leg fell off again this afternoon."

"Well, in that case we should use the bed up here more often. A fine, solid bed like that."

The younger actor sighed in his turn. "Solid indeed. I was

one of those who helped carry it downstairs the last time we used it, and it is my considered opinion it was designed for a race of giants."

"I know. It was a mistake. But we got it cheap."

The younger actor put down the spear he had been playing with and got to his feet. "We will need some kind of a bed. The heroine falls back on it in full view of the audience. But we could take the canopy off this one and saw the posts in half. That would cut down on the weight and make it easier to handle on the stairs." He took the lantern down from its hook. "Come over here and I'll show you." He paused to investigate what lay beyond the muskets. "At least we have plenty of tombs."

Robin knew that it was no use trying to lie still any longer. It would only be a matter of seconds before they found him. He wondered vaguely where he had left his shoes, but perhaps it did not matter. He shook his head to clear it, since it seemed to be a little blurred, and then he sat up with his legs hanging over the edge.

The two men stopped short and stared at him.

"Sirs," said Robin, "I have not hurt anything." He started to get to his feet, still wondering in a woolly sort of way where he had left his shoes. His voice sounded a little skaky but he hoped the actors had not noticed.

The younger actor set the lantern down on the floor. Then he put out his hand and pushed Robin gently back on the bed. It was an unexpectedly strong hand and Robin could not have stood up against it if he tried.

"When," inquired the actor, sitting down beside Robin on the bed, "did you last have something to eat?"

Robin thought this over for a moment. "This morning, I think. Or perhaps it was yesterday." He hesitated, because it was difficult to be quite sure.

The older actor stared at him grimly for a moment and then ran his fingers through his short, graying hair. "I'll take him home for the night," he said finally. "One more will make no difference to Rebecca."

Robin's mouth fell open. There was no reason why anyone should take him home for the night. He was a vagrant and a trespasser, and the greatest possible kindness he could expect from the two actors was to be allowed to leave quietly the way he had come. It occurred to Robin that perhaps the best explanation was that he had fallen asleep after all and was having a dream.

The younger actor, who was still sitting on the bed, had discovered Ruff and was tickling him companionably behind one ear.

"I'll carry him downstairs for you," he said.

He picked Robin up as though he weighed no more than a puppy, and for the first time since he had run away Robin felt the tears pricking behind his eyelids. He was so tired, and the actor's arms were so gentle. He had even taken the trouble to notice that Robin was without his shoes and scooped them up in one hand as they went past.

Ruff leaped off the bed and pattered sedately after, following them through the doorway and down the stairs. There was a lighted lantern hanging from a hook at each landing but otherwise the theatre was dark. It must be very late.

The actor set Robin down at the top of the outdoor stoop and left him to put on his shoes while he went to help the older man untie the reins of his horse. Then he swung Robin up to the front of the saddle with Ruff safe in his arms, and after a friendly wave of the hand turned and went back into the theatre.

"Don't sit so stiffly, boy," said the older man. "Lean back against me and relax. Are you cold?"

"No, sir," said Robin. He looked down on the man's hands as they lay on the leather reins, strong and square and competent. He thought about the actor with the bright hair who had gone back into the theatre, and just thinking about him made it easier to relax.

The horse moved at a gentle trot through the night, following the same road south that Robin had taken with the carter. They passed in under the familiar city gate, but now there were no carts about and almost no lights in the sleeping houses.

"We still have a good way to go," the actor said. "I made the mistake of buying a house at the other end of town. You can go to sleep if you like."

Robin suspected he was already asleep and dreaming. Nothing seemed quite real but the horse, and Robin kept his eyes on the neat mane and the erect prick of the brown ears.

She was a good horse, with an easy motion, and the actor spoke to her from time to time in a pleasant voice.

Finally he reined in at a stable, and Robin slid down obediently to the stone paving. He stood silent, holding Ruff.

"It is only a short walk," said the actor. "This way, boy."

Robin walked with great care, putting his whole attention on the difficult problem of not falling over his feet. They seemed very large and heavy and it was not easy to manage them properly.

"Here we are," said the actor. "And she is waiting up for us."

Robin raised his head and saw a woman standing in a lighted doorway. She was rather tall, with fair hair, and she moved aside to let them pass. The actor said something in a low voice and Robin saw her smile.

"Soup," she said firmly. "Sit beside him on the settle, John, and see that he doesn't fall over. I'll be back in a moment."

The two of them sat on the settle, side by side and saying nothing, while the small flames flickered and crackled on the hearth. Since it was all a dream, Robin saw no reason to bestir himself. But he was glad that Ruff was in the dream, too, because that made it much pleasanter.

She came back, and Robin noticed that her dress was dark blue. "Drink it straight down," she said. "It won't burn your tongue. I tried it to make sure. Straight down, now."

The cup was pewter, shining as silver and with as soft a glow. The soup was very hot but in a gentle kind of way, and it felt as comforting as the voice of the woman. Robin held the cup carefully in both hands and buried his nose deep inside the rim, and it seemed to him that never in his life had he felt so quieted and so safe.

Chapter 9

A sunbeam hit Robin across the nose and woke him. He sat up suddenly in bed and nearly bumped his head against the low, sloping roof.

Ruff was watching from the floor, with his ears pricked up hopefully. When he saw that Robin was awake he leaped up on the bed, ready for play, and Robin gathered him up in his arms and put him back on the floor again. Ruff had never been in a real house and he did not know that beds were not supposed to be jumped on. Robin explained this to him, sitting cross-legged on the floor in his shirt, and Ruff listened carefully.

Still sitting on the floor, Robin tried to think back to the night before. He remembered the fire and the soup and the woman in the blue dress quite clearly. Then he had a vague memory of climbing many stairs and of a boy who moved over in bed to make room for him, muttering sleepily but in a hospitable kind of way. Robin could see two pillows on the bed and an apple core on the chest not far from the brass ewer, so this part was probably correct enough.

The boy had gone now, but someone had been very kind. Robin's shoes had been cleaned and stuffed with straw to get them back into shape, and they were standing neatly side by side at the foot of the bed. His clothes, well brushed, were hanging from a hook in the plastered wall. There was water in the ewer and a clean hempen towel beside it, along with a small square of soap.

Robin washed with great care. His hands were deplorable, and he scrubbed them three times with the soap before he dared to use the towel. It would be a poor return for so much kindness if he left a muddy towel behind him. He saved a little of the water to flatten his hair, which had an unfortunate tendency to stand up straight at the back. He did the best he could with it, but nothing held it down for very long.

He also tried to do something about the bedclothes, but the featherbed defeated him. No matter how much he tried to smooth it out it continued to hump menacingly under the blanket, and he finally folded the blanket back over the bottom of the bed and left things as they were.

Before he took his cap he gave one last look around the room. It was a delightful place, with the sun pouring in through the little dormer window and a bright piece of carpeting tacked on the wall, and he wanted to be able to remember everything when he thought about it later.

Robin went slowly down the stairs, partly because they were rather dark and partly because it was pleasant to stay in the house as long as possible. Ruff raced ahead with the air of one who knew the place well and had gone down the whole two flights before Robin reached the first landing.

Robin recognized the hall at once when he reached it. There was the big oak settle by the fireplace, gay with cushions, the long table with its needlework cover, and the pot of sweet william on the window sill. He thought the room was empty and then he saw a cradle next to the wall, and crouched beneath it a small black cat.

Robin was startled to see the cat. He had been told that cats were very dangerous, bringers of pestilence and compan-

ions of witches, and that no child must ever be allowed near
them. As for Ruff, he was horrified and started circling the
cat while he uttered low, menacing growls. He could not
circle the cat completely because it was close to the wall, but
he did the best he could.

The cat gave Ruff a look of quiet contempt and then ignored him.

Robin hesitated. There was a baby in the cradle, and Robin
could see the tip of its small round nose over the blanket that
sheltered it. He did not like to leave the baby alone and un-
protected with the cat, and so he knelt and put out his hand.

The cat came forward graciously, still ignoring Ruff, and
Robin put out a tentative finger and tickled it behind one ear.
The cat arched itself and then began to purr, so that Robin
could feel its whole body vibrate with delight. It was likely
that this was not a dangerous animal after all, and Robin
spoke to Ruff, telling him so.

"And how will you have your eggs?" said a voice over
them all.

Robin fell back on his heels and looked up. Then he leaped
to his feet and bowed.

She was an old lady, small and brown and with eyes as
bright as those of a marsh tit. Her way of moving was quick,
too, like a bird's, and she cocked her head to one side as she
looked at him.

"Very pretty," she remarked judicially. "I doubt if they
do it any better at Court. And now how will you have your
eggs?"

"Eggs, madam?" said Robin.

"Eggs, sir."

It was clear to Robin that he was being teased, but he did

not know what to do about it. So he bowed again and waited, and the old lady relented.

"My daughter-in-law," she said, "left instructions that I was to give you three eggs. You may have them roasted, fried or poached, as you wish. My own advice would be to have them poached. The water is boiling and much less can go wrong with a poached egg."

He followed her mutely into the kitchen and she waved him to a stool.

"I am no cook," she said. "Never was. Never expect to be. However, there is nothing very complicated about an egg. I hope you enjoy eggshells," she added, peering into the bowl. "There seem to be a few of them here and there. I believe they are nutritious."

Robin put his hands on his knees, since there was nothing else to do with them, and watched her as she worked. Robin's grandmother had died when he was very small and he remembered her only vaguely, thin as a leaf and crumpled among her furs. Her hands were heavy with rings and she seldom spoke, except to give orders that someone always leaped to obey. Her voice had never sounded happy and her room was always dark.

Robin had supposed that people were always like that when they grew old, and he could not adjust himself to the old lady who was poaching eggs. She seemed to be doing it fairly successfully, too, in spite of her rude comments about her own cooking and in spite of the fact that she was paying remarkably little attention to what she was doing. The cat came into the kitchen and wound itself around her shoes, and the little room was full of sunlight and the good smell of pepper.

"Eat it, boy, while it's hot."

The eggs sat on a chunk of bread, white and gold and very handsome, and Robin ate them hungrily but respectfully with a wooden spoon. Meanwhile he wondered what he ought to do. He could not leave the house until he had found the master and mistress and thanked them for their kindness of the night before, to say nothing of the breakfast he was eating now. But he was not clear how to ask for them, and he was not clear about the old lady either. She was obviously not a servant. Perhaps she was the baby's grandmother.

This seemed a safe opening and he tried it.

"I do wish," said the old lady, turning around with the peppermill in her hand, "that you would stop calling me madam. It makes me nervous. My name," she added, "is Mrs. Knell."

This, then, must be the Knell household.

She had at last found a place to put the peppermill, wedging it precariously between a salt box and a wooden pastry board. "Nor," she continued, "am I the baby's grandmother."

She gave the peppermill a vigorous push and dislodged the pastry board. Robin leaped forward and caught it just in time. "However," she went on, "the children call me Grandam." Robin handed her the pastry board. "Thank you," she added.

"The eggs were very fine, Mrs. Knell," said Robin.

"If you want my daughter-in-law," said the old lady, smiling at him, "you will find her in the garden. Her name is Heminges."

Robin paused uncertainly, trying to work this out.

"She is my daughter-in-law by her first marriage. Her present husband is John Heminges, the actor, and a good man he is. I live here because I like them all, and an old woman gets lonely in a house all by herself. They have four children," she added helpfully. "As you go by, just give Joan's cradle a push with your foot. She likes to rock."

Robin was glad to be given clear instructions and a definite occupation. After expressing his gratitude for the eggs, he went back into the hall and gave the cradle a careful and thorough rocking. Joan was asleep, so it made no real difference to her, and Ruff stayed in the doorway in case the cat was anywhere about. Then Robin settled his cap on his head and went into the back garden to find Mrs. Heminges.

It was a small garden, enclosed by a brick wall and bright in the sunlight. There were some berry bushes in one corner, along with what had evidently been a standard rose until someone forgot to prune it, and the garden beds were a riotous mixture of parsnips, marigolds, broad beans, rosemary, cucumbers, lettuce, larkspur, onions and mint. Robin had never seen flowers and vegetables all mixed up together, but they seemed to be enjoying each other and doing well. In the ivy on the wall there was an old kettle tied up with string, with a deserted robin's nest inside it.

Mrs. Heminges was kneeling at the end of a row of cabbages, with her kirtle tucked about her knees and with what appeared to be one of her husband's hats on her head. She saw Robin and waved to him in a friendly manner.

"Good morning," she said. "Do you like cabbages?"

Robin had not expected this and his carefully prepared speech went out of his head. "Why, yes," he said. "Yes, Mrs. Heminges."

She smiled at him. "Then you must stay for noon dinner. No one in the house cares much for cabbage, my husband especially. But I enjoy it, and if you will stay to dinner there will be a good excuse for serving it. Boiled, with a little vinegar and pepper, it should go well with yesterday's beef." She smiled at him again, giving him a confused sense that he was doing her a personal favor by staying to dinner.

"I plant them, you know, and no one eats them. I sometimes think there is a family conspiracy against cabbages and turnips. It does not extend to strawberries and gingerbread."

Robin sank on his heels in the row beside her. "They are fine cabbages," he said, fingering one of the thick, veined leaves. "Much better than the ones we grow in Suffolk."

"You come from Suffolk?" she said. "It is beautiful country up there to the north."

Robin said nothing. Then he knew that he ought to account for himself, after all the kindness she had shown him. "I have come to London," he said finally. "My father and mother are dead."

Mrs. Heminges frowned and for a moment she said nothing either. Then she cut the cabbage neatly from its stalk with a swipe of her short knife and got to her feet. She tilted back her hat and glanced toward the house.

"The whole family seems to be coming to meet you," she remarked.

Robin looked in the same direction and saw what seemed to be a whole troop of little girls. He backed away slightly and then realized that there were only three. They all had blue eyes and their mother's fair hair, and they all stared at him intently.

"This is Alice," said Mrs. Heminges. "My oldest."

Alice, who looked about six years old, dropped him a curtsey and then gave him a sidelong glance through her hair. Robin bowed to her and she giggled.

"My next," said Mrs. Heminges. "Judith."

Judith was perhaps three and armed with a doll, but she also managed a curtsey. Robin bowed again.

"And Seena," said her mother. "We christened her Thomasina, but no one seems to pay any attention."

Seena looked about two, curly-haired and rather portly. She went to Robin and clasped him energetically around the knees, nearly tipping him over. He looked helplessly at Mrs. Heminges, who gently unwound her offspring and lifted her to her own shoulder, giving Robin the cabbage to carry instead.

"Joan you have probably met already, unless she was asleep. She was born last May." She looked around thoughtfully at her collection of girls. "I would introduce you to Alexander Cooke, my husband's apprentice, but he is at the theatre with John. He is a good lad. We all call him Sandy. He shared his bed with you last night."

Robin suddenly remembered his speech of gratitude and

started in on it. But Mrs. Heminges had gone on ahead, with Seena on her shoulder and her knife swinging from her hand.

Judith and Alice, in the meantime, had discovered Ruff, who sat quietly in a bed of lilies of the valley and enjoyed the attention of the two ladies.

"What is his name?" Alice demanded.

"His name is Ruff, mistress," said Robin. Alice giggled again and Robin looked at her doubtfully. He shouldered his cabbage, glad of something to do, and turned toward the house with Ruff at his heels.

"You may have my doll," said Judith suddenly.

"Thank you," said Robin, adding the doll to the cabbage. It was made of wood and had seen better days, but Robin carried it carefully.

Back at the house he took off his cap and did what he could to be helpful about dinner. He was finally set to cutting up the cabbage, with Ruff at his feet and Seena singing a tuneless song to keep him entertained. Alice helped her mother set the table, and Mrs. Knell, who had greeted Robin quite warmly on his return, sliced the beef.

Finally they all sat down around the long table, with the flowers in the window and the cabbage, hot and buttered, steaming in a large dish. Robin was asked to say grace, since he was the eldest male and in fact the only male present. He was sitting on Mrs. Heminges's right, with Seena on the other side, and they both turned and smiled at him.

Robin looked around the room, from the baby safe in its cradle to the fair head of the mistress of the household as she bent it and waited for his prayer. It was easy for him to say grace, although it was something he had never done before, because the household was so safe and so loving and Mrs.

Heminges had grown the cabbage herself. It was easy to be thankful, and he did not lack the words to say so.

What was not so easy was to keep remembering that in an hour or two he must take his cap and say good-by, and that he and Ruff must go out again into the loneliness of London.

Chapter 10

The dessert was very good. It was milk pudding with currants in it, served with Naples biscuits, and while Robin was spooning up his plateful he did some anxious mental arithmetic. This was the third meal he had eaten in this house, to say nothing of the bed he had been given for the night, and Mrs. Heminges had seen to it that Ruff had a large bone entirely to himself. All that Robin had done in return was to cut up a little cabbage and to retie Joan's bib when it fell off.

He could not very well pick up his cap and walk out the front door with a debt like that remaining behind him.

Mrs. Knell leaned over and offered him the last biscuit on the plate. Robin did not know how to refuse it, but it only added to his worries. Then the old lady turned to her daughter-in-law.

"Did Sandy bring the wood in before he left this morning?"

"Sandy," said Mrs. Heminges, "will not be bringing in any wood this week." She turned to Robin in explanation. "The company is acting out the Wars of the Roses in four installments, one afternoon to each, and it means a great deal of extra work for everyone. This afternoon Sandy will be a messenger, a soldier, a watchman and, I think, the Earl of Richmond, and with all that racing back and forth to change costumes we don't expect him to do any extra work around the house."

Robin saw a hopeful light opening in front of him. "May I bring in the wood?"

"Certainly," said Mrs. Knell promptly. "Why not?"

"Thank you," said Robin.

"Don't thank *me*," said Mrs. Knell, pursuing a final currant on her plate. "I realize, of course, that I am doing you a great favor, but I happen to be generous that way. The woodbox is in the kitchen and the woodpile in the back garden."

There was nothing difficult about bringing in the wood except to avoid falling over Seena and Ruff, who insisted on following him on all his trips back and forth to the kitchen. He tried to figure out how much wood would be needed before the Wars of the Roses were finished and then arranged his armloads carefully into three sections—the heavier logs on one side of the box, the lighter ones on the other, and the smaller branches that could be used to start the fire tomorrow morning in a little pile on top. He squared the edges neatly and swept up the bits of bark he had dropped, and then turned to see Mrs. Knell watching him.

"In the course of a long life," she remarked, "I have seen a great many boys bring in a great deal of wood. But never anything like that. There is one last twig behind the door, I believe."

Robin looked, but there was nothing there. He had a feeling that she was teasing him again.

"My daughter-in-law is making the beds upstairs. You might go and help her since you are in such an industrious mood. Tell her I sent you."

Robin found Mrs. Heminges on the third floor. She had taken Sandy's bed apart down to the crisscross of ropes that held up the bedding, and she seemed glad of having someone to help her shake out the featherbed. It was not a very wide bed and it must have crowded Sandy to have a stranger spend the night with him. Especially when he was working so hard in the theatre.

He mentioned the matter to Mrs. Heminges and she laughed. "Sandy was convinced he had fought the whole war when he came home last night. He played an armorer's apprentice and fought a duel onstage with his master. They fought with sandbags and I gather it was a stirring occasion."

"I saw it," said Robin eagerly. "I was there."

"Did you enjoy the play?"

"It was wonderful," said Robin, thinking back.

"It is an old script," said Mrs. Heminges. "Mr. Shakespeare wrote it before he joined the company. It needs a very large cast but it still plays well, I think."

"I was sorry about the Duke of Suffolk," said Robin. "When he lost his head."

"The wool pallet goes first, and then the featherbed. If

you get them level at the bottom it will be easier to tuck in the sheet." She gave him an approving nod and added, "Mr. Richard Burbage played your duke. He is much younger than he looks onstage."

"A very handsome sort of man," said Robin.

"He is that. And with a very beautiful voice. The whole Burbage family is very interested in the stage. His father, Mr. James Burbage, put up the building you were in. He named it the Theatre and still acts in it occasionally although he is an elderly man now. And Richard's brother, Mr. Cuthbert Burbage, worries about the money." She laughed. "I sometimes think that Cuthbert and my husband are the only ones who do."

"The theatre must be a difficult business," said Robin, getting the featherbed to his satisfaction and looking around for the sheet.

Mrs. Heminges handed him one end. "It's a curious business, at least, and one without much safety in it." She paused. "I am rather proud of my husband. His father was a country gentleman and John came to London to be a grocer. The Grocers' Company is one of the greatest in London, with its own hall and its own coat of arms, and John would undoubtedly have ended as a rich man and one of the wardens in the Company. He has a remarkable business sense. But instead he became an actor, back in the days when Lord Strange was patron of the group, and he will never leave it now. He worries about money sometimes—especially now, with prices going up the way they are—but we own the house and no one can be sure of complete safety in anything. I like a man who loves his work enough to give up both money and respectability for it." She smiled. "Actors are considered not much better than vagrants, you know."

Robin remembered the man in St. Paul's Cathedral and wished he could tell him how wrong he had been.

"John is not the only one. There is Mr. Shakespeare, for instance. Before he joined the company he was a real poet, the kind who gets his work printed. Mr. Field and Mr. Harrison are both very important in the book business, and each of them published a book of his. If you will look in the parlor, you will see the one that Mr. Harrison published on the center table, signed by the author. I haven't read it yet because I don't get much time for reading, but John tells me that both books are quite famous and that Mr. Shakespeare could have been a really important poet. But he gave up that sort of thing when he joined the company, just as my husband gave up being a businessman, and now he doesn't do any writing except, of course, his scripts for the company. If you saw the play yesterday you must have seen Mr. Shakespeare. He had the part of King Henry."

Robin's mind went back to the actor who had picked him off the bed and carried him downstairs. He had not looked like King Henry, and yet there had been a kind of resemblance.

"Does Mr. Shakespeare have very bright eyes and auburn hair?"

Mrs. Heminges nodded. "Now the pillows," she said.

Robin reached for the pillows. "He is very strong," he said, thinking of the safety of those arms.

"All actors need to be strong," said Mrs. Heminges, "and they learn acrobatics, too. Mr. Will Kempe, for instance, belonged to a troupe of tumblers before he joined old Mr. Burbage's company. You must have seen him yesterday too. He played Jack Cade."

Robin wished he had known all these things earlier. He

especially wished he could see Mr. Shakespeare again, to thank him both for his kindness and for having written the play. He would have liked to thank Mr. Heminges, too, who worried about money and yet who was willing to house and feed a strange boy. Perhaps, he suggested, Mrs. Heminges would be willing to convey his special thanks to her husband when he came home that night.

"He won't be late tonight," said Mrs. Heminges. "There was a special inventory last night for some new play, and that delayed him. He and Sandy should be home by sundown. Why don't you stay until then and thank him yourself?"

"I would like to," said Robin. "And perhaps he would take my thanks to Mr. Shakespeare."

"I am sure he will. And the bed looks very well. We make a good team, I think." She went past him to open Sandy's window. "By the bye, I don't know your name."

"Robert." He paused a moment. "Robert Johnson."

His hair was evidently standing up again at the back, and she gave it a brush with her hand as she went by. "Very well, Robin."

No one had ever called him that except his nurse, and he had not thought that he would ever hear it again. It made him feel like a small boy and at the same time it gave him a curious feeling of belonging to someone. That was a foolish way to feel, and he told himself so.

During the afternoon Robin made himself as useful as possible. It seemed to be assumed that he was staying to supper, and he did his best to earn it in advance. But he did find time to slip into the parlor and look at Mr. Shakespeare's book. It was the only book there, lying on the center table in the middle of a small needlework mat embroidered with flowers.

The book was rather thin and did not look as though it

had been read very often, and Robin wiped his hands on his breeches before he opened it. Then he studied the first line.

From the besieged Ardea all in post . . .

Robin read it over three times, but it did not make much sense to him. Probably poetry was not supposed to make sense. He liked much better the lines about the vile bezonians that the Duke of Suffolk had shouted before he died. That may have been poetry, too, but of a different kind and more interesting.

Still, it was Mr. Shakespeare who had written the book, the man who was so strong and so gentle and who noticed everything. Robin put it back in the exact center of the mat with careful reverence. Then he went out in the garden and weeded the gooseberry bushes, which seemed to need it. It did not make much difference now, but they would enjoy the breathing space around them next spring.

The children were all in bed by the time Mr. Heminges and Sandy came home. Mrs. Heminges waited for them in the doorway, just as she had the night before, but this time she greeted a different boy.

Sandy looked about thirteen, a tall, dark youngster with beautiful eyes. He must have worn a straw-colored wig when he played the apprentice and done something to make his cheeks stick out, because he did not look the same at all. He gave Robin a friendly grin and showed no special surprise at seeing him there. He headed at once for the supper table in the hall but was sent out instead to the kitchen to wash. He could be heard splashing and then demanding in a raised voice where someone had put the towel.

Mr. Heminges greeted Robin in a friendly way and then

turned and kissed his wife. Robin had never seen two grown people kiss each other, and he could not help feeling a little startled. He dropped his eyes in case they did not want him to see them, although as far as he could tell they did not seem to care at all.

Perhaps Mr. and Mrs. Heminges kissed each other quite often. There was no reason why they shouldn't, after all, since they loved each other. In fact, as Robin thought it over, it seemed a sensible thing to do.

His speech of gratitude to Mr. Heminges had been carefully rehearsed, but he could not find a proper moment to deliver it. The actor had wandered over to the supper table and was looking meditatively at the salad, which had been cut small and mixed with olive oil and vinegar. Robin had poured the vinegar. There was also a hot leg of mutton on a platter.

"Looks good," said Mr. Heminges. "Hurry up there, Sandy."

There was not much conversation at the beginning of supper, since everyone was too busy eating. But Mr. Heminges remarked that the new gatherer was working out well, and Robin remembered the tall man in the doorway who had held out the box for the pennies. He was glad the man was doing well, since he could not help feeling a personal interest in everyone in the company.

He decided to ask Mr. Heminges what had happened to King Henry that afternoon in the Theatre. Things had not been going well for him the day before.

"I regret to say the king breathed his last this afternoon," said Mr. Heminges. "He was murdered by the Duke of Gloucester." He turned to his wife. "Dick and Will made a fine scene of it, too. Will did that bit about the owl shrieking at Gloucester's birth as though he'd never heard it before in his life, and then Dick lunged at him with his dagger like a devil incarnate. We ought to get a big attendance tomorrow when Gloucester gets the throne and becomes King Richard. There is nothing like a succession of murders and a really strong villain to bring out the customers."

Sandy looked up in brief interest from his plate. "I like that ghost scene tomorrow," he said. " 'Dream on thy cousins smothered in the Tower . . .' "

"You sound singularly unlike a ghost," said Mr. Heminges. "How many times must I tell you to draw a full breath before you start? And keep your voice much more level."

Sandy grinned at him amiably but his thoughts were obviously not on acting. Mrs. Heminges was serving the stewed pears and they had Sandy's whole attention.

"Does no one feed you during the day?" she murmured, as she passed his plate to him.

"He eats all the time lately," said Mr. Heminges, looking meditatively at his apprentice. "No doubt he is building up his strength for the Christmas season."

Mrs. Heminges turned to Robin. "Christmas really is a busy season for actors," she explained. "Apart from the regular work, a great many rich people have private showings at their homes in the evenings and there is the full season at Court."

Mrs. Knell looked up suddenly. She was sitting in front of the fire, sewing, having had her supper early with the children because she believed in eating lightly at night.

"Speaking of Christmas," she remarked, "it is my considered opinion that no one is going to persuade Sandy Cooke to carry any more wood until the season is over." She glanced at her daughter-in-law and then went back to her sewing.

Mrs. Heminges looked thoughtful. "I have been thinking about that, John. Very little is going to be done around the house by either of you until after Christmas, and I don't want Sandy to start worrying about an empty woodbox when he is playing before the Queen. What we really need is another boy in the house for a while, and I think that Robin might be persuaded to stay. He is looking for work in London, and he could keep on looking while he stayed here and helped out a little. It would only be until after Christmas."

Robin sat very still, scarcely daring to breathe.

"Where would he sleep?" asked Mr. Heminges. "The house is rather full already, Rebecca."

"He can sleep with me," said Sandy, looking up briefly from his pears.

Mrs. Heminges shook her head. "The bed is too narrow for two. And once the season starts you'll be coming in very late and want to sleep in the morning." She paused to think. "There is that long chest in the children's room we could exchange with the short one Sandy has now. If I put two featherbeds on top it should be fairly comfortable to sleep on." She turned to Robin. "Would you like that?"

He stared at her wordlessly. It would be like coming out of the ice of winter into full spring, with a bank of primroses growing where the snow had been. He did not know what to say, but Mrs. Heminges apparently felt she had been answered. She smiled at him and gave Sandy another helping of pears.

Chapter 11

After Robin had said his prayers that night, he thought the whole matter over carefully.

Mrs. Heminges had put a heavy blanket over the two featherbeds on the chest and then had started to worry that he might roll off. She had tucked him in tightly before she left, although he had assured her that he would be very careful. She had given Ruff a square of matting made of plaited rushes, and Ruff was already asleep beside the chest with his tail curled in and his paws crossed.

The room was very quiet and it was hard for Robin to believe that he was in the middle of London.

When he was small he had sometimes played a game with himself in which he pretended he was living with a real family, with a father and mother and brothers and sisters. They went on picnics together and told stories around the fire at night, and his father and mother both kissed him before he went to bed. As he grew older he stopped playing this game because he knew it was a childish one.

Robin told himself it was important not to start playing the game again in his mind. The Heminges family was not his family and he had no claim on any of them. They were letting him stay for a little while because Sandy was working nights, and it was Robin's business to make himself useful and keep out of the way as much as possible. Also, he must

remember not to take a second helping of anything, because his room and board did not rightly include second helpings.

It was fortunate that Ruff was such a good dog. Anyone would be glad to have him in the house. And every day Robin would look for work, so that if Mr. and Mrs. Heminges wanted him to leave before Christmas they would feel free to tell him to go.

It was all quite clear in Robin's mind, but he found it difficult to make things work out that way.

For one thing, Mrs. Heminges did not seem to realize that he was a stranger in the house. She took his shirt away to wash for him and gave him an old one that Sandy had outgrown to wear instead. The shirt came back mended, and the rip Robin had made in the cuff hardly showed. But Sandy did not want his old shirt back again, and so Robin ended up with two shirts instead of one.

The following Sunday was cold and windy with a reminder of winter coming on, and Robin wore both his shirts to church to keep warm. Mr. Heminges wore his gray quilted doublet and Mrs. Heminges her high-crowned hat, and Robin held himself as erect and dignified as possible to take his part worthily in the family procession.

The parish church of St. Mary's was just down Aldermanbury Street, and on one side of it was the neatly clipped grass of the churchyard. The family went to the churchyard first because little Mary Heminges was buried there, and her mother laid a bunch of late garden flowers by the small stone before they all went inside.

The interior of the church was cool and gray and reminded Robin of his own parish church back in Suffolk. But instead of the tombs of the Wakefields, with effigies in armor, there

were monuments to merchants along the walls with one especially splendid tomb nearer the altar. The sermon sounded
familiar, too, and Robin listened to it carefully. His Aunt
Isabella had always expected him to repeat the various headings
and subheadings afterward, and perhaps Mr. Heminges might
expect him to do the same.

But after the sermon Mr. and Mrs. Heminges lingered to
speak to their pastor. Mrs. Knell shepherded the children
home, all of them chattering like a flock of sparrows, and
Sandy, a determined host, took Robin around the church to
show him all its glories. Sandy was not a Londoner, having
been born in Kent. But he was full of local pride and considered London the finest city on earth, with St. Mary Aldermanbury the finest parish within its walls.

Sandy showed Robin the tomb of Sir William Eastfield,
who had once been mayor of London and must have been
a very rich man. He had not only managed an expensive mon-
ument for himself, but he had given the parish the five bells
in the church steeple and had built the great water conduit
down at the corner of the street.

Sandy did not let Robin linger by the tomb because he
had a greater wonder to show him. He dragged his friend
into the cloister and there, fastened on the wall so that no
one could steal it, was the shankbone of a giant. It was five
times the size of any ordinary person's, and Sandy said it belonged to one of the giants who lived in London before the
Romans came.

Sandy knew a great deal about the Romans. A friend of
his had been passing through Spittlefields while the brick-
layers were digging clay and had found a little Roman pot,
shaped like a rabbit, with the mouth of the pot between its

ears. Sandy knew a lot about both Romans and giants, and he told Robin many interesting stories about them as they walked home together in the Sunday calm.

They arrived to find Alice and Judith having a fight. It was something about a stuffed horse and Robin never did find out what had begun it. But he was truly appalled, since he was not accustomed to the occasional wars that come up in family life and therefore took them much too seriously.

Judith finally swatted her sister over the head, holding firmly to the hind legs of the horse and yelling at the top of her voice. Robin longed for Mrs. Heminges to return and do something. But Sandy walked over to them calmly, pulled them apart, gave them each a mild spank, put the horse out of reach and then ignored them both.

Sandy's method seemed to work since Alice and Judith played together amicably for the rest of the afternoon. They usually did, which was one of the reasons why Seena had attached herself so devotedly to Robin. She felt left out of things, and Robin made a special effort to see that she was happy. He carved her a small horse out of a chip of apple-wood that he found in the woodbox and Seena carried it around in her apron and sang to it at intervals while she clutched Robin firmly with her free hand.

The next morning Robin was commandeered by Mrs. Knell, who did the marketing and who wished Robin to carry the basket. Mrs. Knell shopped with a large hat tied under her chin and the light of battle in her eyes, and every storekeeper in the neighborhood knew her well. She went all the way to East Cheap for her meat, and then fought the butchers there so vigorously that she might just as well have chosen an opponent nearer home.

She had four different fishmongers, none of whom she

trusted, and would slap the fish on the counters by their tails to see if they were fresh. She bought oysters with as much care as if they were diamonds, although oysters were cheap in London and always newly caught, and the apothecary to whom she went for her ginger and nutmeg and almonds cringed when he saw her coming.

Robin, carrying the basket, looked at these transactions with respectful awe, but his private opinion was that Mrs. Knell was enjoying herself. And since the apothecary winked at him as they were leaving, it was quite possible that the apothecary was enjoying himself, too. All the people of London seemed to do battle when they shopped. It gave them the same excitement they got out of going to theatres and cockfights.

Mrs. Knell had a friend in the south part of London whom she visited occasionally, and the next time she went she took Robin with her. The friend was a widow also and lived in a little brick house that had been built by a rich man for the relief of worthy widowed gentlewomen. There were six of these little houses, and the six ladies who lived in them had to promise never to shout or swear. The widows who lived nearest the street had to hang out a lantern at night, with the other four ladies supplying the candles. They had a well for their water, which no one else was allowed to use, and none of them could marry again.

Mrs. Knell felt that her friend led a tragic life, full as it was of enforced virtue, and she used to go once a week to play cards with her. The rich merchant who made the rules had not said anything about cards, and Mrs. Knell and her friend played gleek and primero with a well-worn deck and argued endlessly. It sometimes seemed to Robin that Mrs. Knell made up her own rules as she went along.

Ruff accompanied them on all these expeditions, partly because he never allowed himself to become separated from Robin and partly because he did not wish to be left alone with the cat. The cat treated Ruff with a cold contempt that was hard on a friendly dog, and Ruff was careful to avoid her until one day he caught a mouse. This achievement seemed to give him a kind of confidence, especially when Mrs. Heminges stroked him and told him he was a fine dog. That evening he went and sat in front of the fire, in spite of the fact that the cat was there first. The cat made no open objection and after that they sat side by side in the evenings, looking at the flames and getting in everyone's way with their tails.

The fire in the hall was kept roaring, for the days grew colder all the time, and Robin carried in load after load of wood. There was talk from time to time of using seacoal in the fireplace instead, but seacoal was a shilling a bag, while Mr. Heminges had a friend just north of town who supplied wood very reasonably.

Sandy reported that seacoal was used in the fireplace of the rehearsal hall where they were working, night after night, on the Court productions, but he added that they were all kept busy enough not to need any fire at all. The Master of the Revels and his staff were all worriers, and apparently they woke in the night and brooded over everything that might go wrong when the plays were presented before the Queen. They had Sandy worrying, too, after a while, and he began to talk in his sleep.

All the plays at Court that year were being given by the same company, and while it was a great honor it was a great responsibility, too. Mrs. Heminges stayed up each night for Sandy and her husband, no matter how late they were, and there was always something hot waiting for them. Robin was glad he was there to do Sandy's work for him and pictured his roommate acting in some great rôle in the palace at Whitehall while Queen Elizabeth applauded. Sandy merely remarked that Mr. Phillips's apprentice was working much harder than he was, and that anyhow you had to expect that sort of thing at Christmas.

Just before Christmas Day it snowed and the city lay white and beautiful until the carts churned ruts in the roads and the people began to throw out their eggshells and meat bones. The parish raker, who knew Robin quite well by then, was bitter about this habit and did not like the snow. But Robin loved it and came home with his feet soaked, having taken part in a snowball fight with three strange boys in Silver Street. Mrs. Heminges made him take off his shoes and stockings at once, and they steamed pleasantly in front of the kitchen fire.

All over London the bells were ringing until the whole air seemed to be filled with their sound. In St. Paul's Cathedral the great organ joined the Christmas celebration, while the white-robed choristers sang anthems that soared to the highest vaulting of the arched roof. The children were bringing home greens, the apprentices had bits of holly stuck in their caps, and the shops did a brisk trade in raisins.

Mrs. Knell was carried away by the excitement of the season and decided to make some marchpane, and Robin helped by blanching the almonds and pounding them vigorously in a stone mortar. Mrs. Knell mixed the nuts with sugar and rosewater and spread them on wafers to bake, and when they emerged from the brick oven she was in her glory. She had a series of molds from which she made her decorations, and when the little birds and animals were gilded they were finer than anything that could be bought in the shops. Robin's piece of marchpane was topped with what appeared to be a heraldic bird, or at least it was like no bird he had ever seen before, and he put it carefully away so that he could keep it forever.

By this time the rehearsals at the Office of the Revels were being called much less frequently, because the officials were worrying more about costumes and properties and less about the actors as the final days drew near. Sandy and Mr. Heminges were able to be home occasionally in the evenings, and Mrs. Heminges always treated this as a special occasion.

Robin loved these evenings the best of all. Ruff and the cat sat together in front of the fire, the cat purring while Mrs. Knell sewed. Robin pulled up the long table and Sandy brought out the little square box with holes in it that was used for roasting chestnuts. The Christmas ale was already on the fire, seething and hissing with the crab apples bobbing cheerfully around in it.

Robin was sent to get the four songbooks that were kept in the chest in the parlor, and he loved the very look of them. He already knew half the songs by heart and was learning all the rest. He carried the treble, with Sandy the tenor, Mrs. Heminges the alto and Mr. Heminges the bass.

Robin had been trained in part-singing, since, like dancing and fencing, it was an accomplishment that every gentleman was expected to know. But Sandy and Mr. Heminges seemed to have forgotten more about it than Robin had ever learned, and he had to be alert to keep up with them. The four of them tried every sort of arrangement, sometimes abandoning Mr. Byrd's book of songs entirely to work out some idea of their own. Mr. and Mrs. Heminges alternated in playing the family lute for the accompaniment. Mrs.

Heminges was saving up to buy a viol for her husband, but this was supposed to be a secret.

They stayed up very late, laughing, and the fire burned low because no one remembered to put any wood on it. Mrs. Knell fell asleep in a corner of the settle with a bit of red wool in her hand, and the crickets on the hearth shrilled even louder than the purring of the cat.

Mrs. Heminges did not like crickets and did her best to get rid of them. She said they ate holes in the woolen stockings and aprons that were hung in front of the fire to dry, which was quite true, and she and the cat pursued them endlessly.

Robin did not like to disagree with Mrs. Heminges. She was the sun around whom the whole household revolved, and he had the deepest respect for all her opinions. But he liked the crickets and he always associated them with the firelight and the laughter. Whenever he came in at dusk and heard the crickets singing, he knew with a lifting of his heart that he was home again.

Chapter 12

The twelve days of Christmas came and went, and the carols and the holly and the fat Christmas goose went with them. The snow melted but the days were gray and cold, with plumes of smoke lifting into the sky from all the London chimneys.

The plays at Court were a great success and the company was worthy of the high honor of having been asked to play before the Queen. Sandy reported that Queen Elizabeth had laughed at all their jokes, including one of which he still did not see the point, and that she had a deep, lively laugh for such an old lady. He also recalled that she wore a diamond almost as big as a pigeon's egg, but most of his memories were of things that had gone wrong backstage. They usually did, because the Grooms of the Chamber did not really understand costuming problems and the Revels workmen never gave the scenery time to dry.

After Twelfth Night, Sandy and Mr. Heminges began to return to normal. The two final performances before the Queen were not scheduled until Shrovetide, and the evening performances at the houses of various noblemen were beginning to slacken off. Sandy began to go to bed at a reasonable hour and Mr. Heminges was able to have a quiet supper at home.

Robin knew that it was time to leave. There was no possible

reason why he should stay with the Heminges family any longer.

Whenever there had been a free afternoon during the past month he had gone out to look for work. Once he had thought he was successful, when he applied as gardener's boy in one of the big houses along the Strand. But the head gardener was not willing to take him on until spring and that would have been too late.

There had been an opening also in an apothecary shop in Knightriders Street. The apothecary had been building up a kind of delivery service among the doctors in the neighborhood and wanted a boy as his messenger. But he finally gave the position to a nephew who had come up from Somerset and needed work. It would have been a good position for Robin, because the apothecary had an herb garden behind his shop and Robin could have done all the gardening for him. He was a kind man, fond of jokes, and he was obviously sorry to tell Robin that the position had been filled.

Robin found one other opening, in a bakeshop on Thames Street. The business had been doing well since it was near the wharves and the river shipping, and the baker had decided to take on an extra boy. He told Robin to come down the following Thursday and he would give him a final answer.

Thursday was cold but clear, with the first blue sky since Christmas, and Robin thought it might be a good omen. He dressed himself with special care and then stopped in the hall to tell the family where he was going.

Mrs. Knell looked up from her mending, which happened to be boring her. Her widowed friend lived on St. Peter's Hill, which was only a short distance from Thames Street, and she announced that she would walk down with Robin and pay her a visit. It was a pleasant day and she had been saving a Christmas pie.

Seena saw them both ready to leave and howled. It was Seena's birthday and up to now everything had gone well. Robin had spent many evenings carving her a little doll out of ash wood, and Sandy had brought home some left-over paints from the Theatre so that he could color it realistically. Sandy had begged them from Mr. Richard Burbage, who liked to dabble in painting, and when the doll was finished it was so handsome that Mrs. Heminges had sewn it a little dress.

Seena clutched the doll devotedly and named it Barker, for no clear reason that anyone could discover, and so far her birthday had been a rapturous one. But it gave her false standards, and when Alice and Judith refused to do her bidding and finally would not play with her at all, she fastened herself to Robin and Mrs. Knell and demanded to be taken with them.

She clung to Robin, howling, and because it was her birthday they gave in to her. No doubt the widow would enjoy a visit from Seena, and Robin could carry her if her small legs gave out before the end of the half-mile walk. Her mother dressed her in two extra petticoats since it was so cold a day, and the three of them set out holding hands with Ruff racing in front.

When they reached Cheapside, Seena demanded to be allowed to look in all the shops. Majority opinion was against her, but Seena was a persistent child. She had not come along merely for the walk, and when they reached Thames Street she demanded to be taken down to the river to look at the boats.

Mrs. Knell and Robin had a weakness for boats, and since

the sun was shining so brightly they could see much merit in Seena's idea. The river was gray in spite of the blue sky overhead, but it gave Robin a lift of the spirits just to look at it.

They walked out on the nearest wharf and looked downstream, where London Bridge arched its heavy load of carved and painted buildings and the water swirled white and angry between the stone arches. Beyond London Bridge lay the great sea-going ships, but nearby at Queenhithe was a forest of smaller boats, with men shouting and boxes and barrels glittering in the sun. The watermen rowed back and forth across the river, their flat boats gay with cushions for the comfort of their passengers and their voices hoarse with quarreling with the other watermen along the river stairs. There were two big theatres on the other side of the river and the watermen had a great many customers.

Robin knew he would not be able to find work with any of the watermen. There were too many of them already, old sailors who had served under sea captains like Drake and Hawkins and who were now trying to support large families by rowing customers across the Thames.

Once, down near Whitechapel, Robin had met a man who offered to try to get him work on one of the big ships, and Robin had almost agreed to go. Then he remembered that there would be no room aboard for Ruff. The bakeshop man, on the other hand, was quite willing to house a dog as long as Robin was responsible for feeding him.

There might be time to go over to the bakeshop now, while Mrs. Knell and Seena watched the boats from the wharf. He turned to tell them where he was going, and just at that moment a man went past and jostled Seena, knocking Barker out of her small fat hand. Seena gave her familiar howl and made a dive for the beloved object.

She was not very steady on her feet, having only recently learned to walk, and the extra petticoats were too much for her. She lost her footing and rolled off the wharf into the water below.

Robin leaped forward, but he was too late to catch her. He stood staring for what seemed to be an eternity with only two ideas in his head. One was that the tide was running and the other was that he could not swim.

The sound of the splash released Robin. He whirled and raced to the opposite side of the wide wharf, in the same direction that the tide was running, and then jumped.

The force of his jump carried him deep into the water, and even the shock of the bitter cold could not drive away the fear that he would not get back to the surface in time. He fought his way up, clutching at the heavy water, and his heart gave a leap of thankfulness when he saw that he was just in time. He grabbed Seena's petticoats as the current pulled her past him, and then with his free arm he hooked himself to one of the posts that held up the wharf. It was dark with slime from the river water sucking around it, and Robin had some trouble holding on until he finally managed to hook one knee around the other side.

After that there was nothing to do but wait. He wished there was some way of lifting Seena out of the water and holding her up in the air. But she would have been just as cold, and in any case her steady howls showed that she was not permanently damaged. He tried to comfort her, telling her that she would be out of the river soon, and then found that her lamentations were all for her lost doll. Robin, who was more worked up than he realized, felt a wild desire to laugh and he ducked his head in the water to sober himself

up. He solemnly promised Seena he would make her a new doll and that it would be twice as good as the old one.

The great merit of Seena's howls was that Mrs. Knell had no trouble finding them both. She had ordered a waterman to row her over and stood in front of the boat waving, in some danger of falling in herself.

The waterman turned his boat skillfully with one oar and brought it close to the post. He hauled Seena aboard, moving his cushions out of the way so that they would not get wet, and then he helped Robin clamber over the side. Ruff was also in the boat, having refused to be left behind, and the waterman seemed a little discontented as he rowed them all to the nearest landing stairs and helped them out of the boat. Still, he was very fair and charged them only the regular price for the river crossing. Mrs. Knell tipped him sixpence, at which he brightened considerably and told them the name of the nearest tavern where they could go and dry out.

Seena wanted to go back to the wharf to see if Barker was still there, but for once the birthday child was overruled. Mrs. Knell carried her to the tavern, talking steadily all the way under her breath, and once she was there took over the place as though she owned it. She announced firmly that she had no intention of going home until they were both thoroughly dry.

She ordered hot milk, and the tavern keeper said, quite honestly, that milk was one thing they never supplied their customers. So she marched next door to a private house and brought back a pitcher full, heating it over the fire in a little saucepan and then pouring some into a tankard for Robin. He was surprised to find that he was shivering, in spite of the

good fire and a large blanket around him, and he was very
glad to have the milk.

Mrs. Knell took a tankard of ale herself, just to be com-
panionable, and as she lifted it she looked over to Robin and
her bright old eyes warmed. "A toast to you, sir," she said.
"And you deserve it, boy."

They arrived home in good order and it was as though
nothing had ever happened. Mrs. Heminges found Robin an
old pair of shoes that had once belonged to Sandy, because
his own had been set too close to the fire as they dried and
the leather was cracking. She did not say anything, but when
he bent to put them on she kissed the back of his neck. And
they had a dish of olives with supper, although olives were
a shilling a pint.

After supper Mr. Heminges went into the parlor to do accounts. He never did them at the Theatre, because he liked
all the bills and lists to be near him, and he did not do it in
the hall because conversations disturbed him. There was a
little brazier in the parlor, and he was able to spread all his
papers out on the center table, close the door and be left to
his own devices.

Mrs. Heminges went into the parlor to speak to him and
was there for some time. Robin and Sandy had played a
whole game of chess on Mrs. Knell's old board before she
came out again.

She left the door open behind her and told Robin that
Mr. Heminges wanted to speak to him for a moment.

Robin knew very well what Mr. Heminges wanted to talk
to him about, and he wished he had managed to see the bakehouse man that afternoon. He had forgotten the matter
of looking for work entirely, what with the excitement of

Seena falling into the Thames, but he would do it the first thing tomorrow.

"Yes, sir," said Robin apologetically, standing in the doorway.

Mr. Heminges looked up. "Close the door, please. And then come over here and sit down."

The nearest stool was piled with the objects that had been taken off the center table and Robin took them into his lap. He sat down, holding the flowered mat and Mr. Shakespeare's poetry book with some care, and waited.

Mr. Heminges bit the feather on his quill pen and glanced at the book. "Mr. Shakespeare has brought us a new script," he said suddenly. "It is a very great piece of writing, finer by far than that book you are holding. But it is theatre poetry, not book poetry, and he will never get any credit for it." He frowned and Robin looked sympathetic. His conscience was clear on that subject at least, and Mr. Heminges had not yet brought up the matter of the bakeshop.

"There is not much we can do except to be grateful for each script he brings us and give it the production it deserves." He looked at his pen thoughtfully. "We are casting now."

Robin could not see what connection this had with him. Still, it was interesting and he waited respectfully.

"It takes a large cast and we shall need a certain number of hired actors. There will be plenty to choose from. London is full of them and there is never enough work to go around. They are professionals and will do their work in a satisfactory manner." He looked at Robin. "Still, we work very closely, as a unit, and we like to choose our extra actors from people who know how to work with us. It takes a great deal of patient, intelligent, day-to-day co-operation to be a good actor. It also takes physical dexterity and a cool head."

He paused and looked at his pen. Then he glanced up again at Robin. "You have those qualities, you know. That was quick thinking today, down by the river."

Robin stared at him. His mind was still on the bakehouse and it was hard to readjust himself.

"We cannot offer you a position as an apprentice. It would not be fair to the boys we have now. But if you would like to stay in my house for the rest of the winter and work at the Theatre in return for your room and board, I can give you the kind of training you would need to become a professional. We have the best company in London, and if we recommend you, any other company would take you in. Can you fence?"

"Yes, sir," said Robin. "A little."

"And dance?"

"That a little, too."

"And you are obviously well trained in music. Does the idea interest you, Robin?"

"Sir," said Robin, and then stopped helplessly, trying to think of a way to put it. "Sir, it would be wonderful. There is nothing I would like better in the world than staying here, and I will do my best in the Theatre."

Mr. Heminges nodded. "It is not an act of charity, you know. We cannot afford that in our business. But you have the makings of a good actor."

Then he smiled, and his face was charming when he smiled. "Moreover, Robin, we all enjoy having you here. Seena is not the only one who would be sorry to see you go."

Chapter 13

Robin went to bed that night with his head full of dreams about being an actor. He tried to be grave and sensible about it. Probably he would have only a small part in Mr. Shakespeare's new play, an apprentice in a blue wool cap or a serving boy in a leather apron. But in the back of his mind he could not help feeling that they might wish him to take the part of a knight, with gilded armor and a jeweled sword, bowing his plumed head before some grateful monarch.

He went to sleep with the applause of an excited audience ringing in his ears, knowing quite well he was being a fool but enjoying himself nevertheless.

When Sandy was told the news the next morning he showed a warm interest in the career of his fellow actor. Sandy did not have a part in that afternoon's play, which was about a local murder and required only a small cast, and he offered to bring Robin's costume home with him after the morning rehearsal if Mr. Heminges would lend him the horse.

"It will be a heavy costume," said Sandy, "and it will take you a day or so to get used to the weight."

Perhaps it was armor, after all, and he would be a knight. Robin raced through his work around the house and then lingered by the front door waiting for Sandy to arrive. When he came, the top of his dark head could be seen over the curve of a heavy bundle that was fastened with cord. It was some rich heavy stuff, the color of garnet. Not armor, certainly, but perhaps the costume of a lord.

Sandy settled down to his noon dinner, which had been kept hot for him over the kitchen fire, and Robin swept a place on the floor so that he could roll his costume out and look at it. He unrolled it reverently and found that it was stiff with embroidery and had an intricately brocaded front. But there seemed to be a great deal of it, and Robin stared at it for a full minute before he realized what it was.

"It's a woman's dress!" he said.

Sandy looked up in mild surprise from his slice of hot mutton. "Of course it is," he said, and reached for an extra piece of bread to go with his gravy.

"But I can't wear women's clothes," said Robin, his mind groping with the problem.

"Why not?" inquired Sandy, reaching for a pickle. "Something wrong with them?"

"Of course not," said Robin earnestly. "Not in themselves. But I'm not a woman."

"Everyone else in the company wears them," said Sandy. "And they're not women, either."

Robin thought this over for a moment. He knew quite well that the company was made up of men and boys, but there was surely something wrong somewhere. He thought back to the play about King Henry and was willing to admit that the witch might have been played by a man. And that might be true also of the wicked Duchess of Gloucester. But, he wondered, how about the queen's lady-in-waiting, the one with the narrow hands who moved like music?

"That was Sam Gilburne," said Sandy, loosening his belt and leaning back comfortably. "He is Mr. Phillips's apprentice. And Mr. Pope's boy played the queen."

Robin's mind struggled to adjust itself. "Mr. Heminges," he said cautiously. "Did he ever wear anything like that?" He looked out of the corner of his eye at the garnet velvet, spread in lavish folds along the floor.

"Hundreds of times," said Sandy, "and he still does. There's not a member of the company who hasn't worn skirts over and over again. And if you think there is anything easy about it," he added, "you are quite mistaken. You have to learn a different way of walking and holding your hands, and your skirt will be held out by curved whalebone that is harder to manage than a fisherman's net. I didn't bring your hoops home with me, but you can try them on Friday when we go to the Theatre for rehearsal. Would you like to put the dress on now and see if it fits?"

Robin drew a resolute breath. "Which end do I start from?"

"It can't be expected to fit very well without its underpinnings," said Sandy, leaving the table to come and assist his stricken friend. "You ought to have an under-petticoat, very close fitting and tightly pleated, and then a farthingale with cane or bone hoops. That would take up the extra length in the skirt. In the meanwhile stand up straight, Robin, and don't look so discouraged."

"I feel discouraged," said Robin, his head emerging disconsolately out of the top of the velvet. "There is too much of this thing. If I add hoops and a petticoat I shall never be able to walk at all."

"Walk!" said Sandy. "Your part calls for you to dance."

Robin stood weighted down by the garnet folds and regarded his friend in horror. "No one," he said decisively, "could possibly dance in this."

"It will be shorter when the hoops are attached," Sandy assured him. "Although a little heavier, too, of course. But don't worry. It will come easier with practice."

"Do you mean to tell me," demanded Robin, "that the average girl goes to a dance wearing a thing like this?" His respect for the female sex had always been high, but he could feel it going even higher.

"Well, of course you're playing a Court lady, so the velvet is heavier than it sometimes is and there will be the weight of the jewelry. But Queen Elizabeth wears something like that and she is in her sixties and can dance a galliard with the best of them."

"She is a very remarkable woman," said Robin feelingly. "All women are remarkable."

"They wear corsets, too," said Sandy. "Whalebone, wood, even iron, and then the bodice very tightly laced. We're not expected to do that, especially if we are doing any doubling. It takes too long to get out of the costume."

"I am glad to hear that," said Robin. "Very, very glad." He gave an experimental kick, and the velvet rose up in folds about him. "If I have to do a dance in this thing I hope it will be something slow, like a pavane."

Sandy paused in the work of extricating his friend from his costume. "No, my lad," he said. "It won't be a pavane. The customers don't like those stately old dances. It will be the lavolta."

Robin had heard the name. It was one of those new dances that had come in from Italy. His dancing master had informed his aunts that it was not the kind of dance that a gentleman learned.

"By rights it should be done with a partner," said Sandy. "But I'll show you the basic step as we do it in the Theatre. You know the capriole?"

Robin shook his head.

Sandy suddenly went up into the air in a kind of curved leap, beating his feet together before he came down. "That is the capriole. Then you turn the body with two steps, spring high and pause with the feet coming together again."

He illustrated, and Robin watched with awe. He had never seen anything like it except in the meadows in early spring, when the young lambs leaped into the air and cavorted like acrobats. Robin had never been able to understand how the lambs could do it, and he felt the same thing about Sandy now.

He tried to imagine attempting it himself, encumbered in the folds of garnet velvet on a large stage while thousands of people watched. His heart sank until it seemed to be somewhere in his heels.

"Don't look like that," said Sandy. "You'll have time to practice."

"Are there any lines to say?" asked Robin despairingly.

Sandy looked thoughtful. "I think not. You are one of the nieces of someone named Signior Placentio, and you are going to a ball at the house of someone named Lord Capulet. It's a big social affair, and everyone in the company will be onstage in one part or another. I'm to play a serving boy in that scene, and then later on I am someone named Balthasar. It's one of those Italian stories, full of murders. Your dance comes rather early in the play and you can go home afterward if you like."

Robin stared bleakly at his costume. "I suppose," he said, in tones of foreboding, "that you showed me only the basic step. There is probably more to the dance than that."

"Oh, yes," said Sandy. "Backward and forward and so on. But it is more a matter of memory work than anything else."

"Memorizing I can do," said Robin. "But jumping—" He fell silent.

"I shall take the afternoon off," said Sandy decisively, "and show you how it goes." He went out in the kitchen to lay in a small store of apples for himself and could be heard explaining to Mrs. Knell that they were needed in the cause of a new theatre production. Then he and Robin went up to the third floor, nearly closing the door on Ruff who had followed them anxiously, and Sandy stretched out on the bed while he explained the whole thing with diagrams sketched in the air.

By suppertime there was a neat pile of apple cores on the floor beside the bed and Robin had found a whole series of muscles that he did not know he possessed. But he had managed to solve both the leap and the kick, and although Sandy said frankly that he was not doing them the way a girl would be expected to, it was at least a beginning. Robin then brought in Sandy's share of the wood, to show his gratitude, and his dreams that night were of swordsmen who turned suddenly into goats.

The next morning Robin went out into the garden and practiced among the deserted cabbages and a few wintry flower stalks. He kicked and turned and jumped industriously, all the while counting time under his breath. Mrs. Heminges brought him out a bowl of soup but said nothing, and he kept up his practicing until noon.

Sandy was home for dinner and brought the whalebone hoops with him. He was due back at the Theatre that afternoon and had made the long trip out of pure kindness.

As Robin had feared, it was much worse working with the hoops. He tried to remember Queen Elizabeth, who did difficult dances just for the pleasure of it, and she an old lady and hampered with diamonds.

He then attempted to do the dance with both the dress and the hoops, and at this point Mrs. Heminges interfered.

"Robin," she said gently, "the world will not fall apart if the dance is not perfect by Friday. Calm down, boy."

"I am calm," said Robin. But this was hardly true.

"You will have a partner to help you, you know. He will be a good dancer and you can rely on him, especially on the turns. Do it again now and let me watch you."

Robin, despairing, did it again, and Mrs. Heminges leaned on her broom and watched him.

"That is really very well done," she said. "But don't try to push the hoops as you move. Leave them alone and they will swing with you. And take much shorter steps, Robin."

Gratefully he took her advice, taking shorter steps and feeling calmer already. It was chiefly a matter of rhythm, really, like using a scythe in long grass. An experienced mower knew how to relax and let the scythe do the work, and the same thing was probably true in this case.

Moreover, on Friday he would not have the management of his skirt to worry about. Costumes were too expensive to be worn at rehearsals, and Robin had been allowed to practice in his only because Mr. Heminges had made special arrangements with the man who had charge of the tiring room.

They had all been very kind. The least he could do was to get that last turn right. He wiped his forehead and started counting again under his breath.

Chapter 14

The Theatre looked deserted in the gray light of early morning, with the trampled grass empty of people and a drift of dirty snow on the north side of the building. If Robin had been alone he would have hesitated about going in. But Sandy pushed the stage door open confidently, and Robin saw that the place was already full of people. They were yawning but they were there.

It was the first time Robin had seen a group of actors off-stage, and he watched them with deep interest. They looked, however, just like anyone else. All of them were in street clothes, with heavy quilted doublets to keep out the January cold, and most of the younger ones wore earrings.

Robin looked around for Mr. Shakespeare, because he had worked out a careful speech of gratitude and wanted to deliver it as soon as possible. He finally found him out on the main stage, standing by a post with one foot on the base of the painted column while he talked to Mr. Richard Burbage. He was balancing a manuscript on his knee and waving his hand in a wide sweep that took in the whole of the stage. He and Mr. Burbage were both talking at once.

Robin thought the two men had the liveliest faces he had ever seen, even counting Mrs. Knell's. Mr. Burbage was the handsomer of the two, as magnificent in his gray doublet and breeches as he had been in the silks and velvets of the

Duke of Suffolk, but on the other hand Robin loved Mr. Shakespeare better.

He hesitated, not wishing to interrupt what was evidently an important conference, and Mr. Shakespeare saw him. Robin had not expected to be recognized, but Mr. Shakespeare beckoned him over, said he was glad to see him again and introduced him to Mr. Burbage. Mr. Burbage gave him a pleasant nod and Robin bowed deeply. He then drew a long breath and tried to remember the opening sentence of his speech.

A small, elderly man came over, his head thrust forward anxiously like a turtle's. He saw the manuscript on Mr. Shakespeare's knee and reached out a protective hand for it. "Mr. Shakespeare, sir," he said, "that is my script, you know. You all have your individual cue sheets, every one of you. I am the one who holds the book."

"I'm sorry, Simon," said Mr. Shakespeare. "Mr. Burbage and I were just trying to work out the first Capulet entrance. The way it is now, the whole thing is as stiff as a procession."

The bookholder was not to be comforted. "That is a valuable script, sir. It has the licenser's stamp on it. You gentlemen forget and leave things about, and I am the one who would be responsible if it were mislaid. It is a very valuable script, you know." He pried the book out of Mr. Shakespeare's hand and nestled it in his own. "I will read the relevant section to you." He riffled carefully through the bound pages with an expert hand. *"Enter Capulet and Juliet and others of his house, meeting the guests and maskers."* He looked up brightly and waited.

"Thank you," said Mr. Shakespeare. "We may as well start at that point, Dick. It's the most complicated grouping."

The bookholder brought out a little stool for himself. He

sat down on it, laid the manuscript open on his knee and clapped his hands three times. The sound echoed back from the walls of the Theatre, and the actors who had been lounging about came forward. Most of them had rolls of paper stuck in their belts and Robin wondered if he ought to have one, too.

Sandy was unrolling his and Robin looked over his shoulder to see the opening lines.

> Strike, drum.
> Where's Potpan?

"The word *drum* is my cue," Sandy whispered. "When I hear it I come on stage with a napkin over my arm and say, 'Where's Potpan?' I'm supposed to be one of Lord Capulet's serving boys and we're getting dinner ready for the guests at his ball. We don't have our lines memorized until Monday, so we're allowed to carry our cue sheets this morning. Excuse me. I have the first speech."

Robin realized he would not be entrusted with a cue sheet of his own since he had no lines to say. But he would have liked to have some badge of his profession, something that he could stick competently into his belt. He looked around for Mr. Heminges and saw him standing nearby disposing of a group of boys.

"Jackie," said Mr. Heminges, "on my right, as my wife. And Gil, as my daughter, on my left. Robin, you belong on the other side of the stage. You are one of the guests we are advancing to welcome."

"Yes, sir," said Robin, hurrying to obey. He was reluctant to leave the sheltering company of Sandy and Mr. Heminges, and the empty expanse of stage that he had to cross made him feel rather lonely. Then he saw that Mr. Shakespeare was one of the actors on the other side and went and stood behind him, having found a sheltering rock in a rather confusing world.

Sandy had darted out on the stage, with a harassed look and someone's scarf over his arm for a napkin. "Where's Potpan?" he demanded, and his voice, which had seemed all right a moment ago, suddenly sounded hoarse from too much shouting.

Mr. Heminges strode forth, surrounded by his group of boys, and Robin moved forward with the actors on his side of the stage. Mr. Heminges was talking in a rather loud voice, teasing the ladies about having corns on their toes, and Robin was so startled it took him a moment to adjust his thinking. He had forgotten that Mr. Heminges was no longer himself, but someone named Lord Capulet. Mr. Heminges would never have said a thing like that.

The booming, cheerful, rather stupid voice went on, welcoming them all to the Capulet house. Then the two groups split up and began to arrange themselves about the stage, and Robin could see they were following some kind of a pattern. It was probably a familiar one that was often used and he concentrated on staying out of everyone's way. At the same time he tried to look alert and intelligent, like a happy guest at the house of a nobleman.

"Foot it, girls!" shouted Lord Capulet in his big, hearty voice, and Robin realized with a sinking heart that it was time for the dance to begin.

A tall boy in blue took Robin's hand and put his own right foot into the first position for the dance. Robin remembered just in time not to bow, decided not to curtsey either, and put his own foot into the same position. He began counting under his breath, very low so that no one could hear him.

The opening steps were simple ones, and Robin and his partner were able to remain in the same position on the stage. Perhaps everything was going to be all right after all. But then they changed positions with the next couple and Robin had to move backward. He was afraid he might knock into someone and could feel himself getting rigid, which he knew was a mistake.

He tried to relax, as Mrs. Heminges had told him to, and lost track of his counting. He missed his partner's turn on the swing and stumbled, nearly bringing the tall boy down with him. Robin tried to collect himself, but by now he had hopelessly lost the beat of the dance. Then he tried to hurry so as to catch up with the others, gripping his partner with a sweating hand, and they crashed headlong into the couple in front.

The dance came to a standstill and there was a moment's complete silence.

Robin stood in the center of the stage and waited to be ordered out of the building.

"What we probably need," said Mr. Shakespeare, breaking the silence with his pleasant, relaxed voice, "is some music. It is very difficult to keep the rhythm without music." He walked downstage and picked up a treble viol that someone had propped against the corner post. "Suppose we try it again."

A large man with curly brown hair had been sitting next to the bookholder, watching the scene with his chin propped in his hand. He got to his feet and gently removed the bookholder from his stool. Then he reached for a *viol-da-gamba* and sat down on the stool himself with the heavy instrument between his knees.

"What shall it be, Will?" he asked.

"Anything in three-quarters time. Try 'The Lovers in the Rye.'" Mr. Shakespeare struck a note and then stopped. "Henry," he said, "change places with Christopher, please."

Robin's partner stepped back and another young man came forward. He had large, cool hands and took Robin in a firm hold that was very comforting.

The music began. It was a gay tune, very well played, and it seemed to lift the dancers up and carry them along with it. Robin's partner moved lightly but firmly, almost like part of the music, and Robin could feel himself being caught up in the same rhythm. His feet were as sure of themselves as they had been during the final day of his practicing among the cabbages, and they finished on the exact beat as the music ended.

Robin looked devotedly at Mr. Shakespeare and then waited to be scolded. But the actors apparently seemed to feel that the incident was closed, and the scene went on. It consisted of an argument between Lord Capulet and one of his more quarrelsome young relatives, and Robin could not help being pleased when Lord Capulet succeeded in outshouting his kinsman.

Then the mood of the scene changed entirely. Mr. Burbage was bending over the hand of the boy they called Gil and speaking to him in a low, urgent, caressing whisper. Gil answered, and Robin thought he had never heard such a beautiful voice in his life. Mr. Shakespeare must surely enjoy hearing his lines spoken as beautifully as that.

He glanced over at Mr. Shakespeare, who was not smiling. Instead he was chewing the end of his finger and frown-
ing slightly.

"Gil," he interrupted, "just what is Juliet saying at this
point?"

"It's a sonnet, sir," said Gil, returning to a more normal
tone of voice. "And very beautiful," he added solemnly.

"Thank you," said Mr. Shakespeare. "But Romeo and
Juliet are not merely reciting a sonnet. What are they really
saying to each other?"

Gill paused to think this out. It took him quite a long time
and everyone waited patiently.

"Well," he said finally, "Romeo wants to kiss her. That's
what is behind all his talk about pilgrims. And she doesn't
want him to. Or at least she says she doesn't." He paused
thoughtfully. "But I expect she does, really. She is teasing
him a little for being so excited, but she is getting a little excited, too." He paused again. "Very excited. Very stirred up.
Juliet is always in a hurry about things."

"Suppose you try the lines again," said Mr. Shakespeare,
and even Robin could see a difference this time. The first
time he had heard only the sound, but now he heard the
meaning.

The big man who had played the *viol-da-gamba* had come
up behind Gil and was standing with his hands on his hips.
"Don't fall in love with your own voice, Gil," he remarked.
"Fall in love with Romeo." Then the tone of his own voice
changed suddenly. "Madam, your mother craves a word
with you."

"What is her mother?" asked Mr. Burbage rather anxiously.

"Marry, bachelor, her mother is the lady of the house."

Robin perceived that they were going on with the play. He would have liked to stay onstage and see how things were coming out, but Lord Capulet was vigorously saying good night. Robin could hear his big, sleepy voice—"Come on then, let's to bed"—as he himself turned and went offstage with the other guests.

Sandy had to stay in the Theatre until the rehearsal ended because he had another part toward the end of the play, and he and Robin went and sat down on the back stairway. Mrs. Heminges had given them two meat pasties wrapped in a clean napkin in case they should grow hungry during the morning, and they ate them both. Robin had not expected to become hungry in so short a time, and he searched the napkin hopefully for stray crumbs.

"It's the worry," Sandy explained. "Actors eat as much as ditchdiggers."

"I was worried enough," Robin admitted. "And I had good reason to be. But they were very kind."

"Not all actors are kind," said Sandy. "I know a boy in one of the other London companies who was beaten with a strap because he left out one word in a line. But men like Mr. Burbage and Mr. Shakespeare remember their own beginnings. They know you get tense when you're new to the work and that when you fail it's not necessarily for lack of trying. They are always gentle with beginners. But get drunk, or talk back, or be late to rehearsals and you'll wish you had never been born."

Robin abandoned his search for crumbs and licked his fingers thoughtfully. He could hear onstage a squeaky voice saying something, and then in answer a fat, female sort of voice that nevertheless sounded like the large man with the *viol-da-gamba*.

"That would be Thomas Pope," said Sandy, listening, too. "He plays Juliet's nurse, and you won't be able to recognize him when he's dressed for the part. He's talking to Will Kempe, who is playing Peter."

Robin had heard of Will Kempe even in Suffolk. He was the greatest clown in England, the special favorite of Queen Elizabeth, and all the country people knew his name and repeated his jokes.

Robin listened carefully for the squeaky voice again. "Peter must be a very important rôle," he said.

"It's a very small rôle," said Sandy. "He will do well to get half a dozen laughs in all. The Nurse is the big comic part in the play."

"Then I suppose Mr. Pope is much more important than Mr. Kempe," said Robin. "He must be, if he gets bigger parts."

"They are both shareholders, like Mr. Heminges and Mr. Shakespeare, and they all work out the casting together. There is no such thing as anyone getting all the big parts. Gil, for instance, is rehearsing as Juliet this morning, but he will carry a spear in this afternoon's play and not have any lines at all."

"I'll never be good enough even to carry a spear," said Robin despairingly. His sins of the morning had returned full force now that there was no longer any meat pie to distract him.

"You did very well," said Sandy reassuringly. "You were quiet and followed directions, and you didn't run around asking silly questions. Everyone has a little trouble the first time onstage, and they all knew you were trying."

"But suppose I do something wrong the afternoon the play opens?"

"You won't," said Sandy. "Just keep practicing and get used to the costume. They will let you keep it at home until the last possible minute. Only be careful of it. Those costumes are fearfully expensive and we use them over and over again." He got up and brushed the crumbs from his knee. "Enter Balthasar, Romeo's faithful servant, with a torch and a mattock, whatever a mattock may be."

He sauntered off with a backward wave of the hand, and Robin wondered if he could ever hope to be so splendidly casual about things. Perhaps if he went home at once there might be time to do a little practicing in the garden before dinner. That last step before the turn needed a great deal of attention.

He looked around for Ruff and found him sitting outside on the back stoop, watching the horses and yawning politely. Robin had been a little doubtful about bringing his dog to the Theatre, but Mr. Heminges had said it would be all right and fortunately Ruff had excellent manners.

They walked home together over the frozen brown grass of Finsbury Fields. The sun had come out, warming the back of Robin's neck, and after a little while he began to whistle.

He whistled the whole of "The Lovers in the Rye" and it seemed to him that it was a very fine tune. Perhaps he would not do so badly after all.

Chapter 15

The great day dawned cold but clear. Robin leaped out of bed and leaned anxiously out the window in his shirt but he could not see a cloud in the sky. He had been fearful there might be an east wind, bringing snow, and had worried about it at night after Sandy was asleep.

Robin found it nearly impossible to choke down any breakfast, and Mrs. Heminges finally sent him out into the garden to split wood. This calmed him down somewhat and made him hungry enough to eat his noon dinner properly. But he became so restless immediately afterward that it was generally agreed he would be better off going to the Theatre. He would arrive too early, but at least he could reassure himself that the building was still there.

Robin knew he would be too early and so he took the long way around, going along Cheapside to Cornhill and then up Bishopsgate Street. It was a good route to take because he could look at the playbills the company had fastened up to advertise the afternoon's play. The notices looked very fine on the posts, with *Romeo and Juliet* printed in large black letters that could be seen a long way off.

A great many of the people who hurried by did not stop to read any of the playbills, and this struck Robin as incredible behavior. It was beyond his understanding how anyone in town could have private business on a day like this.

As soon as he passed the city gates Robin could see the

actors' flag against the sky, proud and gay and confident. No doubt the actors in the Rose theatre on the other side of the river were flying a similar flag, but surely no one would want to visit the Rose when he had a chance to go to the Theatre.

Robin hoped there was nothing important going on that day in London that might keep anyone away. He wanted the place crowded with the customers packed in as tight as herrings and a great roar of approval going up for everything the actors said and did. The last play had not gone over very well, but this one would make up for everything.

He slid into the Theatre and found the backstage area almost empty. The heavy tomb of the Capulets, complete with family crest, reared itself up somberly, and next to it was the new bed that had been bought especially for the production. Mr. Heminges had finally decided it would be a wise investment, since the company was always needing beds, and it looked very fine with its heavy wine-colored coverlet. But, as Mr. Heminges said, it would need a great many pennies from the customers to pay for it.

Out front old Mr. Coker was sweeping off the stage, hurrying to finish before the customers began to arrive and could see him. He was a spry old man who had worked in the Theatre for years, and he went into all the corners with the energy of a housewife chasing mice. He was especially thorough about sweeping the areas where the actors were going to be killed—Mr. Will Sly as Mercutio and Mr. Richard Cowley as Tybalt. He told Robin that Mr. Cowley's black velvet suit would show the dust even more than Mr. Sly's turquoise satin. The area that surrounded the tomb was going to be strewn with rushes, because Juliet would be wearing white when she stabbed herself and it was difficult to keep a white costume tidy.

The theatre gatherers came in and went to station themselves at the various collection points, since the audience always came early when the play was a new one. Robin longed to stay out front and try to estimate how big the crowd was going to be, but he knew that he was an actor and should not appear onstage until the proper moment. So he backed away and nearly stepped on Mr. Simon Purdy.

Mr. Purdy was the bookholder and had been with the Burbages in the Theatre nearly as long as Mr. Coker. He was gripping the manuscript of the play that he had taken away from Mr. Shakespeare the first day of rehearsal, and he was wearing his spectacles in case the weather took a turn for the worse and the light began to fail. He greeted Robin pleasantly, considering he had nearly been stepped on, and remarked that there would probably be a good turnout.

Robin said he hoped so. His attention had been caught by a large piece of paper mounted on a board behind Mr. Purdy's head. Its neatly inked columns carried a list of all the scenes of the play, with the order of entrance of all the actors. Robin's eye flew over the familiar names and there, quite close to the beginning, was "R. Johnson." There he was, right in the midst of them all, and he read it over twice to make sure.

He then remembered that he ought to go and see about his costume. It had been brought back to the Theatre yesterday, carefully wrapped and tied, but something might have happened to it since then. A wise actor always checked his equipment carefully.

Robin went up the stairway two steps at a time and arrived

breathless in the tiring room. His costume was safely there, hung on its proper peg and with a small feather fan and some paste jewelry laid out with it. The tireman was busy collecting a pile of pillows, and Robin wondered mildly why he was doing that. Still, he could get into his costume without any help. It had become very familiar, and he had even grown rather fond of it now that he was accustomed to taking shorter steps.

"One more pillow should be enough for the stuffing, I think."

Robin looked up, hearing a familiar voice and expecting to see Mr. Pope. Instead he saw a huge old lady in a vast blue skirt, with a coif on her head as white as any barn pigeon. Then she winked at Robin and he could see that it was really Mr. Pope after all. But it gave him a most peculiar feeling.

He turned back to wrestle with his own farthingale, developing a morbid conviction that it would fall off during the dance, and was very glad when Sandy came over to help him with the fastenings. Nearby, young Sam Gilburne was kicking off his shoes and humming under his breath. He seemed calm, but Robin suspected he was not. He had found that his own hands were beginning to shake.

The tireman came over to help him with his wig. Robin had forgotten that he was wearing a wig, and he stood very still while it was being fitted. It would be bad enough if his farthingale fell off during the dance, but his wig would be even worse.

The room was full of actors by now, and the tireman and his boy had to be everywhere at once. Robin tried to picture what it was like during a performance at Court, with high officials arguing and the great Queen waiting outside, and he told himself he was lucky the play was not being given at Whitehall. He told himself he was extremely lucky, but his hands remained clammy and he did not dare wipe them on the folds of the garnet velvet.

From somewhere came the sound of a trumpet, three sharp blasts. It was the signal for the play to begin, and Robin's heart gave an uncomfortable jump and moved into his stomach. His dinner was there already, and the two did not get along well together.

He decided that he would sit down, to steady his legs, and he edged his way over to the staircase. He moved down it and sat carefully on the bottom stair, well to one side so that he would not be in anyone's way.

Mr. Augustine Phillips, who was acting both the Chorus and Friar Laurence, strode past him with a long purple cloak around his brown Franciscan robe, and Robin knew there was no escape. The play had started.

He tried to listen to Mr. Phillips's voice, but all he could hear was his own heart knocking against his ribs. Two actors stood waiting for their cue, leaning on their swords, and

Robin wondered what they were thinking about. He hoped their minds were not the blur that his own had become.

Mr. Pope made his way downstairs, taking up twice as much room as anyone else, and steadied his white coif. He looked so solid and so comfortable that Robin nearly reached out to touch him. But then he knew that Mr. Pope could not help him and neither could anyone else. He watched the broad blue back in what was beginning to be almost panic.

A roar of laughter went up from the audience at Mr. Pope's first line, and the sound was as huge as the Nurse but not comforting at all. There must be thousands of people out there, and they had all turned into a single voice that sounded like some wild animal. It would laugh if it was amused, but it would destroy you if anything went wrong.

Robin tried to imagine what it was going to be like, coming out on the stage and facing all those eyes. What if he made a mistake, as he had at the first rehearsal? What if he fell and ruined the play? He could not even remember how the dance began. He tried frantically to remember, but his brain seemed to have turned to lead.

Another group of actors had stationed themselves near him, waiting for their cue. There was Mr. Shakespeare, who was playing Benvolio, Mr. Burbage as Romeo and Mr. Sly as Mercutio, along with two boys carrying torches and four hired actors with masks in their hands. They were on their way to Lord Capulet's party, and in a few minutes Robin would have to get up and go there, too. There was nothing he could do to make time stop moving.

Mr. Shakespeare gave him a friendly smile and Robin stared back at him dumbly. His hands were shaking and his feet seemed to be frozen so that he would never be able to move them again.

Mr. Shakespeare leaned forward and put his hand on Robin's shoulder. "Stand up," he said in a low voice, "and take as deep a breath as you can. Then take another one. Everyone gets stage fright at first, and some of us get it every time the trumpets sound. I do, for one. Pay attention to your breathing and don't think about anything else."

Robin got to his feet. If even the great Mr. Shakespeare was frightened, at least it was not a kind of strange disease that had singled out Robin for special attack. He took a very deep breath, sucking in his stomach and filling his lungs, and held it for as long as he could. Then he took another, concentrating on what he was doing, and noticed that his legs were a little steadier.

Another roar went up from the audience and his heart lurched sideways. "Steady now," he urged himself. "Take another breath."

Sandy went by, giving him a cheerful grin. "Here we go," he said. "And another one tomorrow."

That was true, too. This was not the only play in the history of the world, and Robin was not the only actor whose legs felt limp. In any case, he was not really a boy named Robin. He was the niece of Signior Placentio and he was going to a dance with several charming friends, the lady widow of Vitruvio and Lucio and the lively Helena. There would be a partner waiting and some good music, and all he had to do was to dance and enjoy himself.

He passed Mr. Purdy, who was gripping the script and following each line with a long careful forefinger and then, all at once, he was on the stage. There was a sea of faces beyond, but Robin did not look at them. He concentrated on Lord Capulet, who was advancing in the splendor of a furred scarlet robe with a smile of welcome on his face.

"Come, musicians, play!" said Lord Capulet, and from somewhere came a lively tune, mostly strings but with a fife in it somewhere. Robin found his partner, and to his great surprise his legs did exactly what they had been trained to do. He could feel them moving forward and backward, rising and falling, with no real help from him at all. Nothing seemed to go wrong, and when the music stopped the roof had not fallen in.

Robin drew a deep breath, and this one came naturally instead of having to be thought about. He stole a glance into the audience and saw with great satisfaction that the house was full. He drew another deep breath and even began to enjoy himself in a cautious kind of way.

Juliet was talking to the Nurse and that meant the scene was nearly over. Robin was almost sorry. He liked being out here on the stage, taking part in a play, and he was especially pleased with a large man down front who was standing with his mouth open and following every word that was being said. Robin could not imagine why he had ever thought the audience was a wild beast. They were wonderful people.

The scene was over. As they all went offstage, Robin passed Mr. Phillips, coming on again as the Chorus to introduce the next part of the story. Robin knew the plot already but he was too excited to take off his costume and drop back into the everyday world again. Perhaps Mr. Purdy would not object if Robin stood by him a few minutes and watched the show.

Mr. Purdy paid no attention and Robin found a position by his left elbow, where he could see what was going on without being in anyone's way. Mr. Phillips handed his purple cloak to the tireman's boy so that he could turn into a friar again, and Mr. Burbage went onstage followed by Mr.

Sly and Mr. Shakespeare. Robin could see that the chart over Mr. Purdy's head was vitally important, with all the exits and entrances that the play seemed to need.

Then, in a little while, Mr. Burbage was alone onstage. His beautiful voice came to Robin clearly, and it had an excited, caressing quality that sent a shiver down his spine.

It is my lady. Oh, it is my love . . .

He could hear Gil's voice, hushed and thoughtful and like silver, and then Romeo's voice answering. The two voices, the silver and the gold, played a kind of love duet, and over them was the moon that showed through the top of the fruit trees to light Juliet's balcony. Even the actors backstage and Mr. Purdy's head huddled over his script could not break the spell of that ardent youthful music coming from the two lovers.

It was the Nurse's voice that broke it. She shouted suddenly, "Madam!" in that strong voice of hers, and Robin was angry at the interruption. The Nurse did not realize Romeo was there and after a moment Juliet was able to call him back. It was hard for her to let him go, and her voice reached out with such longing that Robin could not help feeling disturbed. He knew their love was going to end in tragedy and it seemed unfair. They were both so young and so beautiful.

Mr. Phillips went by in his brown robe, carrying a little basket in a hand that had suddenly grown old and trembling. He puttered out onstage, and Juliet went upstairs to change into the green dress with the seed pearls that had been laid out for her. Robin stayed in his corner and the play went on.

He had not intended to laugh, since this was a tragedy. But

there was something about the Nurse and Peter when they were together that upset him, and it finally got so that he had a helpless desire to laugh whenever the Nurse came onstage. Just seeing her white coif was enough to set him off and he nearly strangled trying not to laugh out loud. Mr. Purdy turned once and gave him a grim look, which sobered Robin considerably.

Moreover, there was tragedy onstage, for Romeo's friend Mercutio had been killed. It was easy to see how it had happened, with the weather so hot that summer day in Verona and Tybalt so determined to bully him. Mercutio was a brave gentleman as well as a witty one, and Robin was pleased when Romeo fought Tybalt to revenge his dead friend. It was a violent duel, and Romeo was nearly run through by Tybalt's rapier before he ran in under his enemy's guard and killed him. But then things were worse than ever, because Tybalt was Juliet's cousin.

From then on, there was no way that things could right themselves. Juliet's father tried to force her to marry another man, and she drank a potion so that her family would think she was dead. She was too young to have so much trouble, and her voice shook so just before she drank the potion that Robin wanted to rush onstage and stop her. Especially since he knew that the plan was not going to work.

They laid her in the family tomb and Romeo thought she was dead. He killed himself there, in the tomb under the yew trees, and all his love was stilled forever. Juliet found his dagger and followed him, and Robin could hardly see for the tears that were in his eyes. Somewhere up in the galleries a woman was sobbing uncontrollably, and Robin knew just how she felt. They had been so young and so loving, and they had tried so hard.

Sandy came toward him, his face alight and Balthasar's digging tool still in his hand. "Wasn't it fine?" he said. "Listen to the way they're applauding!"

Robin listened but it did not comfort him. He was glad, of course, that the play was a success. But the young lovers were dead, killed in all the glory of their loving, and nothing would bring them to life again. Even when Robin saw Mr. Burbage, still in Romeo's costume, bury his hot face in a tankard of ale it made no difference, and he avoided the Capulet tomb as he went upstairs to the tiring room. It was their foolish family pride that had killed the two most beautiful people Robin had ever seen.

Chapter 16

Now it was three people who left together for the Theatre in the morning and came home to a hot supper at night. It was four, in a way, because Ruff always went with them. The actors seemed to like him, and he was careful to stay in the same corner so that no one would trip over him. He soon learned the shortest route to the Theatre and walked ahead of them helpfully, his feathery tail waving in the early morning air.

Since *Romeo and Juliet* had been such a success it was presented again the following week. Robin needed experience in doubling, so he was assigned two more small parts in the show. He was given a blue jerkin and a club and allowed to appear in the opening scene as a young citizen of Verona, helping out in the street fight between the Capulets and the Montagues, and in the last scene he had an embroidered doublet and acted the part of a page for the Prince of Verona.

The part of the page was easy enough, since all that Robin had to do was to walk onstage looking alert and respectful. But the other rôle took practice. For one thing, he had to learn to make a very quick costume change, since there was very little time to race upstairs and slip into the farthingale and wig of the niece of Signior Placentio. He was allowed to keep the blue jerkin on underneath, but he was expected to remember all his buttons, not to knock into anyone on the stairs and to arrive at the Capulet ball looking happy and unflustered. It could be done, but only just.

Another difficulty about playing the part of the young citizen was learning how to handle his club. Robin was not supposed to hit anyone with it, but only to look as though he had. He finally realized that behind the apparent disorder of the street fight there was a pattern as precise as a formal dance. The actors did not really race around at random as they seemed to be doing. Each one had his own place in the framework, and Robin learned to handle his club with exact and careful timing.

A further difficulty was an actor named Stephen Furse who was playing Gregory, a servant of Lord Capulet, and who was armed with a sword and buckler. Stephen was a clever actor and a good swordsman, but he took a dislike to Robin since Robin had not been hired by the company in the regular way. Once he even tried to trip him up as he made his entrance onstage. Robin managed to sidestep him, but he kept a wary eye in Stephen's direction for the rest of the scene.

The next day Robin was given a part in a new play to practice. He was to be a young soldier defending a French city in a furious battle. He thought that Stephen Furse would be more annoyed with him than ever, especially since Stephen had the part of a French soldier also. But Stephen merely smiled and offered to give him a little extra training for the battle scene.

They chose a time when the stage was deserted, and Robin loosened his belt so that he would have plenty of room to breathe. He did not know exactly what he was supposed to do, but it undoubtedly would involve acrobatics. And Stephen had been so kind that he did not want to waste any of his time.

Stephen stood under the stage balcony and looked upward.

"The balconies," he said, "will be the city walls. They will be manned by the French defenders, with the watchman standing in the turret on top. The city loses the fight naturally, being French, and the defenders will be forced from the walls until they all fall dead in the moat below."

"The stage is the moat?" asked Robin. He hoped he was wrong, because it was a long way down from the balcony to the stage.

"Exactly," said Stephen. "Now get up on the balcony there and take a fall to the stage. I'll watch to see if you do it right."

There was a backstage entrance to the balcony, but Stephen said it would be quicker to use the rope ladder. It had been left hanging there because Mr. Burbage was experimenting with a new way of reaching Juliet's balcony, and Robin went up it easily.

When he reached the top his worst suspicions were confirmed. It was a long way down to the stage. On the other hand, if he were careful to land evenly on both feet it would probably mean only a slight jar.

"You want me to jump now?" he asked Stephen.

"Jump!" said Stephen in contempt. "A dead man doesn't jump. You must fall back against the edge of the balcony and then drop over, and mind you make it look realistic."

Robin suspected that the only realistic part would be when he landed. He tried to imagine what the boards of the stage would feel like when they struck him across the back of his shoulders, and it was a highly unpleasant thought.

"Are you afraid?" demanded Stephen from below, and his tone was rather unpleasant also.

"Yes, I am," said Robin honestly. He looked down at the stage and the distance seemed to be growing greater by the minute. Still, he had known for a long time that actors had to be acrobats. Stephen was a trained actor and knew all about such things, so it was not likely that he would really hurt himself very much in the fall.

He must use all his will power and try to fall limp, although how he was to go about doing this Robin had no idea. Just to look down at the stage floor made him feel as rigid as the boards themselves.

"Well," he said, and did his best to sound lighthearted and professional, "here I come." He shut his eyes tightly, feeling that things might go better if he could not see what he was doing, and then tried to imagine how it would feel to be a French soldier who had just been stabbed. That part was easy enough. He knew exactly the drained, gone-away feeling the French soldier would have.

Robin decided to stop thinking about it. He set his teeth, dropped forward and sideways, and felt himself launching out into space.

A strong pair of hands caught him by the left leg and jerked him backward. Then he felt himself being gripped by the waist and hauled back to the balcony as though he were a sack of meal.

"What," demanded an outraged voice, "do you two think you are doing?"

Robin opened his eyes and saw the bristling eyebrows of Mr. Thomas Pope. He had seen Mr. Pope shake with comic fury when he was playing Juliet's nurse, but this was a different kind of anger. Evidently they had done something wrong, although Robin was not clear what it could be.

"It was only a joke, sir," said Stephen Furse from the stage below.

"A joke!" said Mr. Pope. "You might have killed him. If you will kindly collect from Mr. Heminges the shilling that is due you for yesterday's performance, we shall not need your services any longer in this theatre."

Stephen opened his mouth to say something. Then he turned and silently left the stage.

"He was only helping me, sir," said Robin. "We were practicing the battle scene."

Mr. Pope was still angry. "We have safety rules in this theatre," he said, "and we enforce them. There has never been a man or a boy crippled on this stage and we are certainly not going to start now."

"No, sir," said Robin gratefully, and Mr. Pope's eyebrows began to settle back into their normal position.

The next morning Mr. Will Kempe took Robin in hand and gave him a brief lecture on balance and control. He reminded Robin of a long, lazy cat the way he moved, and he was as gentle and patient as though he were not one of the greatest acrobats in England. At the end of half an hour Robin was able to begin practicing and in three days' time he took a successful fall from the balcony. Mr. Kempe said he could try it next time without the matting, and Robin could not imagine why he had ever felt the stage was so far away.

Mr. Heminges, who had been standing by watching, remarked that the fall was satisfactory enough in itself but that Robin must remember that he was not playing the part of an acrobat. He was supposed to be a dead soldier.

Robin decided that things would be easier when his fellow corpses were piled about him, but he practiced being dead in all his spare moments. He also found out the best way to lie while he was being dragged offstage by his conquerors, with one arm thrown out and his head lying across it. This was the only way to protect his head, since he was hauled off rather quickly. The stage had to be cleared for the next scene, and the triumphant English got the fallen French out of the way as rapidly as possible.

On the final day of rehearsal, Robin noticed how carefully the actors checked the two cannons and all the muskets. Some years ago another London company had permitted a musket onstage that everyone thought was unloaded, and it had killed two members of the audience. The men of the Theatre took no chances.

That same morning Mr. Cuthbert Burbage gave them a lecture on fire. Someone had been caught smoking a pipe, which was not only expensive but against the rules, and Mr. Cuthbert explained that with so many painted boards and thin fabrics the company could not permit any open flame. Torches and candles were never used backstage, but only lanterns, and there were leather buckets and piles of sand in case anything went wrong. Mr. Cuthbert said that his father had made all these rules when he built the Theatre, and now that James Burbage had died it was even more important that everyone who worked in the great wooden building should keep up the high standards of safety that he had begun.

The play went off very successfully that afternoon, with cannons roaring and men shouting, and Robin died like a veteran. Even Mr. Heminges said he had done well, and the following week he was assigned his first stage duel.

Robin thought he knew a little about fencing, but he had

forgotten that it could not look like an exhibition match on the stage. It had to look like a savage duel to the death, with a long rapier in one hand for attack and a dagger in the other for defense. It had to be completely safe, or the actors would be displeased, and yet it had to look dangerous enough to satisfy the audience. Moreover, Robin was going to wear a white satin suit covered with copper lace, and if he did not keep his costume clean and unmarked he would hear from the tiring man.

Robin worried about his new problem for two days and would have gone out among the cabbages to practice by the light of the moon if Mrs. Heminges had let him. But she said he needed his sleep and she was probably right, because he woke up one morning and could see quite clearly what he was doing wrong. It was not what the audience saw that was important; it was what they thought they saw. If the actor cringed the audience would think he had been struck, even if no blow had really landed; and a rapier could seem to slide in under an opponent's desperate parry when in fact the opponent's weapon was opening the way for it. It was a game of illusion, the whole thing, and the trick was to persuade the audience to let itself be deceived.

Robin tried to explain all this to his fellow duelist, but it seemed that he knew it already. He merely smiled and said that Robin would make an actor yet.

The following week the company tried out a new script, written by a young playwright who had not had much experience in the theatre. It needed a large cast and Robin was given his first speaking part. He was to be the lady-in-waiting of the heroine and had twelve lines to learn.

Robin's mistrust of skirts was outweighed by his excitement at getting a cue sheet of his own, and he stuck the roll into his belt with a fine professional flourish. That evening he sat up late by candlelight to memorize his lines, and he was full of confidence when he arrived at the Theatre the following morning. He knew all the words forward and backward. He also knew how to keep his hands folded, as any decorous lady-in-waiting should, and he would remember to take short steps.

Mr. Heminges took him aside to hear him say his lines, and Robin's self-confidence vanished abruptly. He started off with too much of a rush, lost his breath in the middle of the fourth line and had to stop to catch up with himself. Breath control was as important in acting as in singing, as Mr. Heminges pointed out to him. Moreover, Mr. Heminges expected him to make himself heard at the back walls of the galleries.

Robin tried to stand still and orate, since that seemed to be the only way to make his voice carry that far, and Mr. Heminges remarked mildly that he was supposed to be a lady-in-waiting, not a Roman senator. Moreover, he would have to start making his exit three lines before the end of the speech or else walk the full length of the stage with nothing to do.

Robin hoped to solve the problem by giving the speech more slowly, but that did not work either. Mr. Heminges explained that the show had to end before dark, so that the people could get home to their suppers, and that Robin would be allowed just thirty-one seconds in which to deliver his twelve lines. But they would not worry about characterization this time, Mr. Heminges said, and Robin was grateful for that at least.

As it turned out, he only recited the speech before one audience, because the play was a failure and was never repeated. It had looked well in the script, but something had been missing between the stage and the audience. The miracle never took place that turned two thousand separate people into a single excited listener. All the hard work, the buying of properties, the making of costumes, the long rehearsals had gone for nothing.

Mr. Heminges stayed up late that night, figuring, but when he saw Robin the next morning he merely remarked that this sort of thing happened frequently. There was no way of knowing in advance what an audience was going to like. Even Mr. Shakespeare had once written a play that was not a success. It was about King John, and Mr. Heminges said he was going to try it again some day. Simon Purdy still kept the script in his locked chest, with just the same care as the successful ones.

It was Mr. Purdy who had tears in his eyes when Robin arrived at the Theatre that morning. But his sorrow had nothing to do with yesterday's disaster. He had just discovered that the text of *Romeo and Juliet* was on sale in the bookstores, secretly printed against the actors' will and without their consent.

Mr. Purdy felt that he had betrayed his trust. He kept assuring the actors that the script could not have been stolen and then returned; he had never let it out of his sight. They assured him in return that John Danter, the publisher, must have sent someone to the Theatre to take the play down in shorthand—a new way of quick writing that had recently been invented for no better purpose than to bedevil actors. The company spoke to each other in hushed tones all morning, out of respect for Mr. Purdy's grief, and someone brought him an extra bottle of ale for his noon dinner in the hope that it would cheer him up.

Mr. Heminges said it was difficult to keep a play out of print, especially such a successful one. But he had heard that

Danter's version was not accurate and told Robin to go to one of the bookstalls and get a copy.

Armed with sixpence, Robin set out an hour earlier the next morning, and he and Ruff went to St. Paul's Church-yard, where every book in London was on display. He had no trouble finding *Romeo and Juliet*, for the little pamphlets were set out in a large pile. Robin leafed through the one on top looking for the potion scene, which he had heard was full of mistakes and not at all as Mr. Shakespeare had written it.

"What do you lack?" inquired the bookseller's apprentice, popping his head up from behind the counter. "A copy of the latest play, sir? Learn how to make love to your girl in choice language for sixpence?"

Robin had heard this was one of the reasons the play was selling so well. But he did not want the apprentice to think he was any ordinary customer. He laid down his sixpence and turned with elaborate casualness to the title page, which told the name of the acting company and announced that the show had been getting great applause.

"I have acted in it," he said.

The apprentice looked up with flattering surprise. "You have?"

"Yes,'" said Robin, with what he hoped was suitable diffidence.

"Then you must know William Shakespeare," said the apprentice in awed tones.

Robin said that of course he knew Mr. Shakespeare. He knew all the actors in the company.

"Are you afraid of him?" asked the apprentice.

Robin looked at him in astonishment. "Why should I be?"

The apprentice sighed. "You would be if you had ever tried to do any writing of your own. The man is supernatural. He can do anything with words. Listen to this, from the balcony scene." He leaned over, took the little book from Robin's hand and found the place immediately. Robin did not want to be late, but he composed himself politely to listen.

The apprentice read badly, with no breath control at all and stumbling over some of the words. But there was so much love and excitement in his voice that anyone would have enjoyed listening to him.

As he hurried to the Theatre, Robin thought over what the apprentice had said. Mr. Shakespeare was certainly not a frightening kind of man. If anything he was almost too gentle, and while Mr. Burbage's voice got louder and louder when he was excited about something Mr. Shakespeare's only got quieter.

But it was true that there was a kind of magic in what he was able to do with an audience, and all the skill of the actors could not save a script unless Mr. Shakespeare's kind of magic was there first. Illusion in acrobatics and swordplay could be taught, but building up an illusion through words was something that could probably never be taught, no matter how hard you practiced.

Robin was glad he was a beginning actor and not a beginning playwright. He remembered the young dramatist whose play had failed yesterday and who had gone up into the property room and cried. Actors made mistakes, too, sometimes, but their mistakes did not show so much.

Still, the young playwright who felt so sorry for himself might have taken a look at the pile of bills that Mr. Heminges had shuffled into a neat pile and regarded thoughtfully. There was a bill from the linen draper for the buckram that was used in making the hollow tree behind which the hero had hidden from his enemies. There was a bill from the armorer, for the rental of three suits of mail and some halberds. There was a bill from Mrs. Huckler, who sewed the insignia on the flags, and one from the haberdasher who made the red wig with which the heroine had disguised herself. There was a bill for the gunpowder that had exploded under the trap door, and one from the apothecary for some imitation fruit. And there were the wages that had to be paid all the extra actors, who worked for a shilling a day and did not care what happened to the play as long as they got their money.

Mr. Heminges and the rest had saved where they could, reusing old properties and remaking old costumes. They had used silvered leather, instead of renting all the armor that was needed, and the heroine had worn Juliet's dress with the skirt turned. But the hero had to have a scarlet cloak with gold lacing and a green taffeta jerkin with silver buttons, and it required six lengths of silk for the cardinal's gown. Prices were going up all the time, too, even the price of paint, and paint was used lavishly. Everything had to look new and glittering and splendid when the trumpets sounded for the afternoon show, because the public would not come to a shabby-looking production.

Yet the actors took the failures along with the successes, and nothing seemed to depress them for long. They enjoyed each other's company and they were very easy to work with. Any member of the company was willing to spend hours in the area under the trap door on the center stage, showing a new assistant how the floor signals were worked in that stuffy lantern-lit little space. The silkman might argue prices with them but he always shared a cup of ale before he left, and the armorer invariably brought his whole family to the Theatre to see each new production.

The property maker, who supplied everything from moss banks to devils' eyes, once told Robin privately that he was lucky to be in such a company, but Robin knew that already. He had to work hard and his feet were always cold. But he could not help wishing sometimes that the winter would last forever.

Chapter 17

The days lengthened, and so did Robin. His doublet finally became so short it was difficult to keep his hose up, no matter how he pulled at the points, and his breeches were in real danger of splitting.

Mrs. Heminges said nothing about it, but one morning Robin found on his peg an old suit of Mr. Heminges's, cut down for him and neatly sewn. It was dark green, with flaring shoulders and cutwork in the front, and Robin wore it with great pride, both for its own sake and that of its former owner. Sandy admired it greatly and then offered Robin a pair of his own shoes to go along with it. He claimed they were an old pair, but they were hardly scuffed at all and Robin knew that he had been given a very fine present.

In an effort to make some slight return, Robin took over Sandy's usual task of helping Mrs. Heminges put in the garden. He had not meant to do it for his own pleasure, but he had forgotten how much delight there was in crumbling the cool spring soil. He would sometimes stop digging just for the pleasure of bending down and feeling it between his fingers, and also to give the robins a chance at the worms that were being turned up. The robins had returned to the kettle in the ivy, and they seemed to feel he had been put in the garden for their special convenience.

Mrs. Heminges developed large ideas about the garden that year, having found an assistant who was willing to spend the whole evening talking over the relative merits of leeks and radishes and who spent long hours after sunset spading sections of the garden that had never been spaded before. Whenever Robin could be spared from the Theatre the two of them worked among the neat rows of green. They knew every budding leaf on the fruit trees, and not even the robins were more learned in the ways of worms.

One afternoon when Robin was not acting, Mrs. Heminges gave him a large basket and sent him out to Holborn in the western suburbs. He presented himself at the door of Dr. Gerarde and was told by the housekeeper that Dr. Gerarde was out in his garden. "He always is," she said with a sigh.

The doctor said that he was delighted to see any friend of Mrs. Heminges's and how had the ginger plants fared that he had given her the previous autumn? Robin said honestly they had all been winterkilled, and the doctor's face fell. "Mine, too," he admitted. "Mine, too. However," and he brightened, "I believe that I am going to enjoy a signal success with something quite new that is called the Virginia potato. I will send some to Mrs. Heminges if all goes well. Would you like to see my garden, boy?"

Robin said he would be very glad to see the garden and they went over it gravely, inch by inch. Dr. Gerarde seemed to have a passion for growing whatever was wrong for the climate, and for the past three years he had been trying to rear some cotton seeds that had been sent him from Aleppo. He also had marigolds from Peru and iris from Dalmatia, and something called Turkey corn which would surely ripen if they had a hot summer.

Robin peered at the unpromising little green shoots with the deepest respect. He himself, as a gardener, inclined toward the simple, solid things that flourished in Suffolk, but he was awed by Dr. Gerarde and not at all surprised to find he was writing a book on the subject. He went home with his basket full of roots and cuttings, and safe in his breeches pocket were the wrinkled seeds of something called Indian cress or nasturtium. It had come into Spain from the Indies and had been sent to Dr. Gerarde by a friend of his in Paris. He said he was glad to share the seeds with his other friends, such as the Heminges family, and before Robin left he gave him some detailed and useful advice on the best way to plant muskmelons.

As Robin walked slowly back to Aldermanbury Street, he could see signs of spring everywhere. Every garden was budding out with green, and the early cherry trees were foaming over the brick walls. The birds were all talking at once, and the children were telling their mothers that they could not possibly be expected to wear their heavy jackets any longer. Ruff skittered about like a puppy, and Robin had to whistle to him twice before he remembered to be a sober town dog and stay at heel.

Robin usually loved the spring, and it was not because he was spending it in town that he felt depressed. It was because he knew that in the summer the actors left London. They toured the smaller towns of England, taking along only a few of their most experienced members, and the Theatre would be shut down. Robin tried not to think about it, but he knew that his work at the Theatre would soon be over.

He arrived home to find that Mrs. Heminges had decided to give a picnic. She knew a farmer out beyond Aldgate who had a green slope with a brook running through it. He would let them sit on the grass and supply a pail of milk for the children. It was rather a long way, nearly half a mile beyond the city gates, but they could hire a cart and leave right after church the following Sunday. Mrs. Heminges was convinced that it would be an especially fine day on Sunday.

Mrs. Knell said that her daughter-in-law always got the same gleam in her eye every spring, and, mark her words, the picnic would end up with a great many more people involved than just the Heminges family.

This was quite true, for by the end of the week everyone who worked in the Theatre had been invited. Mrs. Heminges even asked Mr. Purdy, who said he never went on picnics because it was not healthsome to sit on the grass. It turned out, however, that all he needed was a little persuading and the promise of a small cushion.

Mrs. Heminges and Mrs. Knell spent the week roasting meat and baking a succession of pies, and it was as much as anyone's life was worth to go near the kitchen. The two Burbage brothers promised to supply the ale, which they could buy wholesale from the concession man who supplied the Theatre.

Augustine Phillips's wife, Anne, promised to make some of her famous violet comfits for the occasion, the ones for which she would never reveal the recipe. The Phillipses lived on the other side of the river with their two little girls, three-year-old Magdalen and Mrs. Heminges's godchild Rebecca, who had been born last year. Since it was such a distance, Mrs. Phillips persuaded her husband to hire a cart. They got it next door in Horseshoe Court, and Mr. Phillips's apprentice, Gil, agreed to do the driving.

The Phillipses' party expanded to include Mr. Pope, who lived nearby in Mr. Langley's New Rents. Mr. Pope had never married, which he said was no misfortune, but he adopted a succession of children because he liked to have them around the house. They were brought up by his housekeeper, Mrs. Willingson, along with whatever apprentice Mr. Pope happened to be training at the moment.

Mrs. Willingson said she would bring a jar of pickles, as long as there was going to be a cart. They would also pick up Mr. Will Sly, who lived not far away in Rose Alley, before they all journeyed over London Bridge to meet the Heminges family in the picnic place beyond Aldgate.

The Burbage brothers also hired a cart, on account of the ale, although they had a much shorter distance to come. They planned to pick up Mr. Richard Cowley and his wife, who also lived near the Theatre on Holywell Street. Elizabeth Cowley had lost her little son in March and was expecting another child in May. If it was a boy she was going to name it after Cuthbert Burbage, and he was the one who finally persuaded her to come to the picnic.

It made a very large party when they all met together in the farmer's field and started unpacking themselves and the provisions. There were ten people from the Heminges household alone, counting Ruff, and Mrs. Heminges had brought enough food for an army. There were pigeon pies and a whole roast of beef and six chickens and some pig's pettitoes, and buns and cakes and fruit. Everyone had brought something, except Mr. Sly and Mr. Shakespeare who boarded out and did not have kitchens. But they ate as much as anyone, and Mr. Shakespeare carried the farmer's pail back twice to be refilled. This was kind of him since he did not like milk.

The weather was all that Mrs. Heminges had said it would be, and a cloudless April sky tucked itself into the green trees on the horizon. London seemed very far away, and even the birds were country birds with a different kind of song. They flirted their tails and watched for crumbs, and Robin persuaded one to come very near his finger. He did not know its

name because it was a kind he had never seen in Suffolk, but he thought it must be a warbler.

Finally it was impossible to eat any more, and the babies all went to sleep on coverlets spread out under the trees. There was a halfhearted attempt at starting a few games, but the babies obviously had the right idea and the hard-working actors could not resist the soft grass and the gentle hum of the bees. Mr. Purdy sat upright on his cushion and stared owlishly through his spectacles, correct to the last, but all about him were sprawled the recumbent forms of his employers.

Mrs. Phillips and Mrs. Cowley started to discuss bringing up children, and Mrs. Willingson joined them. Robin looked around for Mrs. Heminges, but she was sitting under a nearby oak, looking up at the sky and holding hands with her husband.

Robin did not like to disturb them. But there was a question that must be asked and this was as good a time as any. He went toward them and sat down in the grass a few feet away. This would not disturb them if they wanted to be alone, and if they were willing to have him nearer they could call to him.

"You look very grave, Robin," said Mrs. Heminges. "Is anything the matter?"

"Nothing is the matter exactly," said Robin, coming over and sitting cross-legged in front of the two of them. "But I have been thinking. I know I will not be kept on during the summer, but if I found temporary work somewhere in London do you think I might come back to the Theatre in the autumn when it opens again?" It was not a very strong hope, but at least he had asked.

Mrs. Heminges put her attention on pulling up a blade of grass, and it was Mr. Heminges who answered.

"I am not sure the Theatre will reopen in the autumn, Robin," he said. "It looks very much as though we are going to lose the building."

Robin jerked upright. The possibility had never occurred to him. It was like saying that London Bridge was going to be taken away.

"But you can't lose the Theatre!" he protested. "The Burbages own it. Their father gave it to them when he died." He cast back in his mind for the stories Mr. Purdy had told him of the early days of building the Theatre, how hard Mr. James Burbage had worked to raise the money and how he had even done some of the plastering himself to save the cost of workmen's wages. Surely no one could take the Theatre away from the Burbage family.

"Richard and Cuthbert own the building," Mr. Heminges admitted. "But they do not own the land, and the lease has just expired. The landlord refuses to renew the lease because he wants to pull the building down and put up tenements instead. He says they will bring him more money. Cuthbert has gone to see him nearly every day, but all he has been able to get out of him so far is a quarterly extension."

"It is difficult not to dislike the man a little," said Mrs. Heminges.

"We can probably use the Curtain for a while," said her husband. "It is a convenient location, almost next door, but it was never as well built. The backstage area is inadequate and there is not nearly enough storage space. All those properties of ours and those chests of costumes upstairs—" He sighed. "Apart from not knowing where to store them if we lose the Theatre, all our extra money is tied up in them. Not that we have much extra money," he added thoughtfully. "Will Shakespeare saved up sixty pounds, but he has arranged to spend it all buying a house for his wife in the country. It's an old house, too, and he'll be facing money on repairs."

"His little son died last August," Mrs. Heminges explained, "and he has been trying to make his wife feel happier. I don't grudge her the house, if she wants it, but I wish she would sometimes think of trying to make him happy instead of its always being the other way around."

Robin sat shocked and silent. The surface of life in the Theatre had always been so friendly and so smooth he had not realized this sort of thing was happening, the threat to the Theatre, the death of Mr. Shakespeare's son and probably many other things also. He stared down at the grass, and Mr. Heminges reached over and pulled his ear with an unexpected gesture of affection.

"Don't look so worried, Robin," he said. "These things are not your responsibility. We were talking about your acting career, I think, when we got off the subject."

"Yes, sir," said Robin.

Mr. Heminges meditated briefly. "You have made an excellent start, on the whole. You know next to nothing about the use of your voice, and nothing whatever about characterization. But you are willing, and quick to learn, and you already have a good grounding in music and rapier work. I think I could conscientiously recommend you to anyone as an apprentice."

Robin waited, his eyes on the ground.

"There are no openings, as you know, in this company. But Richard Jones is looking for a boy, and if you like I will mention your name to him. He has had a rather difficult time these last few years, but now he has joined Mr. Langley's new company at the Swan and I think the venture will be a success. Mrs. Jones is a good woman and you will like her."

Robin knew that this was a magnificent offer. The Swan was the huge new theatre that had just been built on the other side of the Thames, much more splendid and much more expensive than either the Theatre or the Rose. Any boy who wanted to become an actor should feel overjoyed at being offered such an opportunity, and Robin told himself that he was very happy about it. But he knew he was not. He dropped his eyes to his shoes and could not raise them to meet Mr. Heminges's kind ones.

He admitted to himself that he had never really wanted to be an actor. He was not like Sandy and Gil, who only came completely to life when they were inside the walls of the Theatre. Robin had enjoyed it very much, but chiefly because he had been with people he loved. It was that he wanted, and not the life of an actor. It was the easy comradeship during rehearsals and above all it was the evenings at home—Mrs. Knell teasing him, Seena bringing him a toy to be mended, the talk around the fire and the jokes they shared.

Robin raised his head. "Sir," he said, "you have been very kind. But I think I will not be apprenticed to Mr. Jones. I think I will go back to Suffolk."

Mr. Heminges's face cleared. "Good," he said. "You are a fine boy, Robin, and all of us like you. But it seems to me that you do not have the right temperament for an actor. You worry too much and you are too hard on yourself. We actors need a kind of easygoing conceit to carry us along. Once we start worrying we lose buoyancy, like one of those little diving ducks along the sea coast if it damages its feathers."

"Speaking of ducks," said Mrs. Heminges, "I should think that Robin would make a successful farmer. He must have some private way of talking to the radishes because they never grew like that for me." She smiled at him and after a difficult moment he managed to smile back. "They have good farms up in Suffolk," she said.

"Yes," said Robin. "Very good farms." He did his best to keep his face looking reasonably happy, but it was not easy. It was not only the fact he was going away. He could not even feel that he was leaving the company safe and prosperous behind him.

"Sir," he said, "will things be very bad if you lose the Theatre?"

"Not in the least," said Mr. Heminges cheerfully. "It was a good location when it was built, but most of the theatre business has been moving to the other side of the river. If we could raise enough money, we might even be able to put up a theatre of our own near the Swan. I have been working on some little sketches, and I think it would be possible to make a much more efficient use of the backstage area than the way we have it now."

"But that would take a great deal of money," said Robin. He knew he worried too much but he couldn't help it.

"True," said Mr. Heminges. "And I would be the first to admit that money is very important. So is having a theatre building and some land to put it on. But none of that affects our most important asset, which is the people who make up the company. I don't mind losing the Theatre if we must, but if we were to lose Burbage or Phillips or Shakespeare—"

"Or you," said Mrs. Heminges, laying her hand on her husband's knee. "I think I hear Joan crying," she added. "Perhaps we should think about getting home fairly soon."

She got to her feet in a single easy motion and brushed off her skirt. She leaned forward to pat Robin's shoulder, just to tell him that everything would be all right, and then she walked off across the grass with the long stride that always made her look relaxed and happy. Mr. Heminges followed her with his eyes.

"I never did anything better in my life," he said, "than the day I persuaded Rebecca to marry me. Did I ever tell you about the year of the great plague, when the theatres were all closed and the actors left London? We had to leave our wives behind, and there was nothing we could do for them except to send our letters and our prayers. Robert Brown's wife died that year in London, and all his children."

He paused. "Rebecca and I had been married five years by then, and there was two-year-old Alice and the baby, Mary. She was born during the plague year, when Rebecca was alone in London, and I never saw her. She died that same year of the plague. There was no money to take her away from London. None of the actors had any money that year. But never once did Rebecca reproach me, or admit she was frightened, or ever forget in any of her letters to say how much she loved me."

He was speaking almost to himself and he sat silent for a moment. "I cannot help holding it against Anne Shakespeare," he said finally, "that she refuses to be a real wife to Will. She says she stays in Stratford for the children's safety, but the boy died in any case. And there is a strength in being together that she will never know. I blame her upbringing and her strict, tight, country ways, but I wish in my heart that he had never married her." He looked at Robin and suddenly changed the subject. "Would you like to help me tidy up the grounds?"

They began to repack and finally all the equipment was put back in the carts. Mr. Sly helpfully drank the last bottle of ale, since he said it would be easier to take it back empty, and the small children had a final drink of milk.

The only one who did not want to go home was Alice Heminges, who had been quietly mapping out a project of her own while the adults slept. She wanted to go to the zoo, which, as she pointed out, was not far away. It was practically on the way home, being next to the Tower of London, and she added pathetically that she never went to the zoo while all her friends were taken there regularly.

Mrs. Heminges said it was time the younger children were put to bed, but that Alice could go to the zoo if she could find someone to take her. Alice looked at Robin, who said of course. He had never been to the zoo but he knew quite well where it was.

They climbed in the cart and rode with the family as far as the city gate. Then they got out and walked south, keeping before their eyes the white battlements of the Tower of London. Robin kept a firm grip of Alice's hand, in spite of the fact she pointed out to him frequently she was not a baby. She was only seven, after all, and he had no intention of losing her. Ruff, who of course had come along, kept an attentive eye on her also.

They found the zoo easily enough, a small house close to the Tower with wooden cages for the animals inside. Robin kept Alice well back, so that she would not try to poke her finger through any of the lattices, and they went on a slow and careful tour of all the cages. There were three lionesses and a huge lion whose name was Edward, because he had been born in the reign of the late King. There was a tiger, a lynx, a chained eagle and something which looked like an enormous hedgehog which the keeper said was a porcupine. The keeper obviously expected a tip, and Robin was sorry he did not have any money.

There was also a wolf, pacing back and forth in its cage and stopping occasionally to throw back its head and howl. Alice did not like the wolf and went back to old Edward the lion, but Robin knew exactly how the wolf was feeling, all alone and shut up in a cage.

Robin's thoughts went back to the great house in Suffolk. It was not, of course, a cage because it was much bigger. But he felt a stir of sympathy for the wolf and, without knowing quite why he did it, he picked up Ruff and held him close in his arms.

Chapter 18

The afternoon show was over and the people were trooping out into the warm spring sunshine. The Theatre gradually grew empty, and finally there was almost no one left in it but Robin.

He had told the actors he was planning to go back to Suffolk and they had all said they were sorry. But Robin knew that boys came and went, and that most of them were soon forgotten. He had not even been a very good actor, and it was not to be expected that any of them would miss him. He would miss them though, much more than he cared to think about.

He hung his costume for the last time on the familiar peg, stroking the velvet of the sleeves. He had worn a ruff with it and carried a small sword. He could not help feeling that if it had been a farthingale it would have been easier to part with, since he had never really adjusted himself to the idea of skirts.

He gave the doublet a small, furtive pat and then told himself not to be foolish. He might not be dressed like a girl but he was certainly acting like one.

If only he were not going away into emptiness! Suffolk was not really empty, of course. There were a great many people in it. But as far as Robin was concerned, everything he loved was in London, and Suffolk was very lonely and far away.

He told himself again not to be a fool and turned to go.

As he passed the glazed window at the head of the stairway he noticed that Mr. Shakespeare was sitting with his back to it, a sheaf of papers in his hand and an inkhorn rather precariously balanced on the ledge. Robin had the curious feeling that Mr. Shakespeare had been watching him, but that was impossible. Mr. Shakespeare was a very busy man.

The window was half open to let in the warm spring air, and outside it the martins were flying. Robin stopped to look at them for he always took a deep interest in martins.

"Do they nest here, sir?" he asked, and then realized that he had probably interrupted Mr. Shakespeare in something important.

"Every year," said Mr. Shakespeare. "It is our sure sign of spring."

Robin pictured the martins coming back next year to find the Theatre torn down and nowhere to build their homes. It seemed sad to him for a moment, and then he knew it would not seem sad to the martins. Birds were not like people. They did not attach themselves quite so tightly to the places they loved.

"They always nest on the north side," said Mr. Shakespeare. "I wonder why."

Robin thought he knew why, and it was a great credit to the good sense of the martins. He began to explain eagerly, as proud of the birds as though they had been friends of his.

"They work like plasterers, sir. They make their nests by flattening the clay up against the wall of a building, and they balance themselves by their tails as they pack the clay down. They can only do a little at a time because they must wait for each section to harden properly, and if they work in the full sun on the south side of a building the heat cracks the clay. So they usually choose the north. It takes a martin about two weeks to get the whole nest built." He paused, thinking of them with affectionate awe. "They are wonderful birds."

"You must love birds," said Mr. Shakespeare.

"I do," said Robin. That was one good thing about Suffolk. It was full of birds.

"It's an interesting thing about loving," said Mr. Shakespeare. "It makes you so clever. Gil loves the theatre the way you love birds, and he has learned more about it in three years than the average person could learn in fifty. I once knew a man in Stratford who felt that way about horseshoes. He said their curve was the most beautiful thing he knew. His wife said he was a fool, but I expect he was nearer the truth than most people."

Robin sat down on the floor and rested his chin on his knees. "I suppose," he said, "that anything in the world is worth loving, birds or horseshoes or theatres or even pigs. I remember once spending a morning watching a white worm. I meant to step on it and then I got interested, and you have no idea how much there is to a worm. But if you step on it, of course, you never know."

" 'Having eyes, see ye not?' " Mr. Shakespeare smiled. "I don't know why love is always pictured blindfolded. It is the one thing that sees clearly."

Robin had a feeling he was going to be impertinent. "What is the thing you love?" he asked.

Mr. Shakespeare did not take offense. "People," he said. "Like your martins, they have their reasons, and I like to find out what they are. When I read a book or an old play, I can see the people moving around behind the pages, waiting for someone to set them free, and that is why I write plays of my own. The words are waiting, and the people. It is only a question of getting them together."

He made it sound very easy, but Robin remembered the bookseller's apprentice who had spoken of him with such awe. The apprentice had wanted to write, too, but the words had not been waiting.

"It doesn't always come to order, just through wanting it," Robin said.

"No, it does not," agreed Mr. Shakespeare. He grinned suddenly. "If it did, I would ask the Creator for the gift of ciphering. I remember the first year I joined the company I was paymaster, along with Will Kempe and Dick Burbage. They thought that no one could know less about figures than they did, but they were quite wrong. So now we let Heminges and Pope do it for us. Apart from everything else, you know, a dislike of mathematics makes for a very unsound financial policy. For instance, if I were reckoning up what the company owes you for your winter's work, I should make it an even shilling a day because I can add shillings. But John Heminges says it should be elevenpence, because you are not a fully trained actor, and he is quite right."

"But I am not owed anything!" said Robin, startled. "I was given my training, and I had room and board."

"That would have been enough if you were going on with an acting career. In that case the training would have been of some use to you. But as it is, we think it would be unfair to accept your services without a reasonable payment."

Robin did not trust himself to speak. It was an extraordinary piece of kindness, unexpected and undeserved, and he did not know how to express his gratitude properly.

He looked down at his hands and suddenly realized that now he could do the thing he wanted most in the world.

"Sir," he said, "I would like to spend it on a present for Mrs. Heminges."

"Surely not all of it," said Mr. Shakespeare. "You will need to hire a horse to get you back to Suffolk, to say nothing of paying for your lodging at the inns where you spend the night. But that will leave you enough for a good present."

"I want something remarkable," said Robin. "Something she can't cut down for any of the children. Do you think she would like a piece of jewelry?"

Mr. Shakespeare gave the matter his whole attention. "I should think that would be an excellent idea," he said.

"Do you know a reliable jeweler?" asked Robin. "Cheapside is so full of people shouting that it gets very confusing if you are looking for something."

"It seems to me," said Mr. Shakespeare, "that this is a special occasion and we ought to go to the Royal Exchange. Suppose I lend you fifteen shillings while the matter is still uppermost in our minds, and we go over and look for something now."

"Would you mind if Ruff came with us?" asked Robin.

"Not at all," said Mr. Shakespeare.

They left word with the stagekeeper to tell Mr. Heminges that Robin would be late coming home. Fortunately he had on his best suit, the one that Mrs. Heminges had fixed for him. The Royal Exchange was not a place for ordinary shoppers.

Mr. Shakespeare was looking very fine in a suit of dark brown velvet, and Robin decided that when he grew up he would wear gold earrings and a small ruff just like his. They had nearly the same length stride, which struck Robin as a remarkable coincidence.

The Royal Exchange was even more magnificent than Robin had expected. It was a large two-story building, with arches, built around a hollow square, and the main floor was crowded with rich merchants who had gathered after business hours to discuss finances and hear the latest news from abroad. They talked of fleets to Russia and the Orient, and most of them had expensive beaver hats and wore jewels. From the snatches of conversation that Robin caught about prices and ladings he could see that he was in the investment center of Europe. Like Mr. Shakespeare, he was not very good at mathematics and he was deeply impressed by men like these who were clearly merchant princes.

Mr. Shakespeare pushed his way through with great firmness, stopping only occasionally to speak to someone he knew, and led Robin to the upper corridor that ran all the way around the building. Here were the shops of the goldsmiths, the glass-sellers, the bookmen, the armorers, the silkmen and everything else that anyone could want, fat with luxury and glittering with newness and splendor.

There were many ladies on the second floor, doing their shopping in a swirl of feathered hats and embroidery and perfume, and it took a determined man to work his way through them. Robin stayed close behind Mr. Shakespeare, with Ruff in his arms so that he would not be stepped on, and it was not until they reached the farthest end that Mr. Shakespeare halted.

Before him was spread out a display of jewels that glittered like a sky full of stars. There were golden chains and cups circled with rubies, pearl bracelets and enameled pins, rings set with diamonds and opals, turquoise and topaz, emerald and amethyst. They must have cost thousands of pounds, but they were certainly beautiful.

There was in particular one little dagger, the hilt lightly chased with a design of vine leaves and the blade as shining and blue as ice. Robin picked it up for a moment, just to see how it felt, and it was born to his hand. He wondered for a fleeting moment if Mrs. Heminges would like to have a dagger. It was so beautiful that she might be able to find some use for it. Perhaps she could keep it as an ornament. Then better sense prevailed and he put the dagger down.

Mr. Shakespeare was smiling at him. "I bought her a book for her birthday once, and she gave it back to me on mine. She knew very well I was the one who wanted it. Still, that would hardly work out in your case. Do you think she would like a chain?"

They looked the chains over, discussing their respective merits, but they all seemed too heavy and too formal to Robin. They would have been all right for Court ladies, dressed up and chattering, but they were not right for Mrs. Heminges.

"Something more feminine," said the jeweler understandingly. He was a small, dark man who was giving his whole attention to the problem. "I believe I have the very thing."

He drew it out from under the counter and held it for a moment in his narrow hand before he passed it over to Robin for his inspection. It was a small enameled chain made of linked roses and daisies, so real that the white curve of the daisy petals could almost have sheltered a bee. It was the right thing exactly, fragile and yet strong, and Robin did not dare to ask the price.

"Eighteen shillings," said the jeweler.

It was less than he had expected, but he only had fifteen.

"I expect we overestimated the cost of hiring a horse,"

said Mr. Shakespeare. "I remember now that a friend of mine got one for eightpence a day and the oats were thrown in. I will get the name of the stable for you." He counted out three extra shillings into Robin's hand. "You can give it back to me when you get your wages."

Robin passed the little heap of coins over, and the jeweler wrapped the chain in a twist of paper so that he could carry it safely in his breeches pocket. Robin took it with a quiet glow. It was exactly right and she was sure to like it.

"I think we ought to celebrate," said Mr. Shakespeare. "I have nothing in particular to do this evening and you are not expected home until late. Suppose we have supper together."

They went to a tavern in Bread Street, called the Mermaid, and sat at a table facing each other. Mr. Shakespeare asked Robin to order the supper, because he was tired of eating out and wanted someone else to do the choosing for him. Robin thought the matter over carefully and then decided on oysters followed by a shoulder of mutton. For dessert they had some little gingerbread cakes, of which Mr. Shakespeare ate seven.

He seemed to be well known in the tavern, and a great many people came up to speak to him. There was a Mr. Heywood and a gentle, thin-faced man whose name was Michael Drayton. Both of them seemed to be very fond of Mr. Shakespeare, a situation that Robin could well understand.

They talked of many things, and Robin could not follow all that Mr. Shakespeare said. But it felt like sitting in the sun. You do not have to understand sunlight in order to enjoy it.

It was almost dark when they finally left the Mermaid,

and the stars were beginning to prick through the sky. There was a moon, too, and Mr. Shakespeare began to hum under his breath as they walked along.

"It's a curious thing," he remarked, "that I can remember nothing about figures. I can remember every ballad that I ever heard."

"Do you know the one about the monstrous pig?" asked Robin eagerly.

"There are two about monstrous pigs," said Mr. Shakespeare and obligingly recited them both. It was the second one that Robin knew.

> Come near, come near, good Christians all,
> Behold a monster rare . . .

Mr. Shakespeare sang vigorously, in a good loud voice, and Robin came in on the third line. They sang the rest of it together, sounding rather well. Robin found that he remembered every word, and it was set to a fine tune.

Mr. Shakespeare also knew the one about the burning of Beckles.

> O day most unlucky! The wind low in sky,
> The water hard frozen, the houses so dry . . .

They walked along slowly, since it was a fine night and there was no hurry. It was nearly midnight when they arrived on the Heminges doorstep, arm in arm by the light of the London moon. They were still singing, and Robin had heard nearly every ballad that Mr. Shakespeare knew.

It had been a wonderful evening.

Chapter 19

Robin had meant to save the chain until the morning he left, but he found he could not wait that long to see if Mrs. Heminges liked it. So he gave it to her the afternoon before. He found her in the garden, which seemed a suitable place, and presented the gift with a carefully worked-out speech of gratitude.

Mrs. Heminges brushed the dirt from her hands on her apron and took the small thing carefully. Her face looked rather like Seena's when she had been given the doll, and Robin knew that he had found exactly the right thing. When Mr. Heminges came home that evening, it was the first thing she showed him.

Since it was Robin's last supper everything was planned that he liked best. There was roast chicken with orange sauce, and a plate of olives, and new wheat bread. There was also something by Robin's place, carefully wrapped in a napkin. He did not know if he was supposed to look at it or not. But when they were all seated they gazed at him expectantly, and he raised one corner cautiously.

The dagger lay there, ice-blue and gleaming, with the vine leaves curling up the hilt. Robin picked it up slowly and cradled it in his hand, and it was even more beautiful than he had remembered.

Sandy explained that Mr. Shakespeare had bought it, but

that it was a present from everyone in the company. They wanted to let him know they were sorry he was leaving, and even Mr. Purdy had contributed twopence.

Robin had a great deal of difficulty eating his dinner after that, and Mrs. Knell said that if he put the dagger out of sight somewhere he would get along much better. He grinned at her and she smiled back at him, and Robin knew that never in his life had he felt such a sense of pure happiness.

His elation vanished when he went upstairs that night and started to get ready for bed. It was not only that he was leaving in the morning and would probably never see any of them again. He had faced that already. But what troubled him was that he had been deceiving them. He had said that his name was Johnson, and he ought not to leave with a lie on his conscience.

After a brief moment of mental struggle Robin pulled on his breeches again, smoothed his hair and went downstairs. Mr. and Mrs. Heminges were sitting together on the settle, as they usually did in the late evening, because he liked to tell her everything that had happened at the Theatre during the day.

"I am sorry to interrupt you," said Robin, "but there is something I must say." He spoke rather quickly, so he could not give himself time to change his mind. "I did not tell the truth when I said that my name was Johnson. It was true about the Robert, but my last name is Wakefield. Sir Robert Wakefield," he added anxiously, so they would have all the facts. Then he looked down at his shoes.

There was a short pause.

"That seems reasonable enough," remarked Mr. Heminges. "I wondered once or twice how you happened to know so much about music and swordplay. It's not usual."

"Yes, sir," said Robin, still looking at his shoes.

"Don't look so sad, Robin," said Mrs. Heminges. "It's not a crime to be a baronet or whatever it is you are."

"It was wrong not to have told you," said Robin in a low voice.

"Not at all," she said. "It saved a great many complications. If we had known your name and where you lived we should have had to send you home at once. As it is, we *are* sending you home at once. The timing is excellent."

She kissed him, to show how clever he had been, and Robin turned and went off to bed. Mrs. Heminges always gave him the comfortable feeling of having done the right thing, even when he knew he had not. With his Aunt Isabella, on the other hand, it was just the other way around.

He decided not to think about his Aunt Isabella. There would be time enough for that later on.

Robin got up early the next morning to do his packing, although there was not very much of it. He hesitated over the little bird made of marchpane that he had saved from

Christmas. It was beginning to crumble and probably he was foolish to keep it. On the other hand, he had a perfect right to be foolish if he wanted to be. He wrapped it in the small piece of cloth that had been around his father's signet ring, and slipped the ring on his finger instead. His hand must have been growing, because the ring fitted exactly.

The horse had been brought around to the front door, and since it was still early, Mr. Heminges and Sandy had waited to see him off. All the family had gathered in the hall when Robin and Ruff came downstairs. Mrs. Heminges was wearing her present and had left off her apron in his honor. Seena was howling rhythmically, and even the cat, normally a cool animal, was emotionally disturbed.

Robin longed to tell them that he would come back to London soon and see them all again. But he knew he would not and so he promised instead that he would write. He would write every week and tell them all the news. Perhaps they would write him back once in a while, and it would be almost like being in London again with the family he loved best in the world.

He turned in the saddle and kept waving as long as they were in sight, and when the house was finally hidden by a turn in the street he felt a strong desire to behave like Seena and howl like a baby. He blinked his eyelashes rapidly and was ashamed of himself.

Fortunately the horse was in a lively mood. He had evidently been given a good breakfast of oats and he needed Robin's full attention. It was several minutes before they came to a complete understanding with each other and then the horse resigned himself to a meek trot, with Ruff keeping close behind.

Robin cut crosstown through the quiet back streets that were only just beginning to wake up for the day, and he did not meet any heavy traffic until he reached Bishopsgate Street. There the early morning carts were coming into town, taking the same route that he and Mr. Huggen had taken so long ago. Robin reckoned up the time and realized with surprise that it was only last autumn. It seemed to him that he had been in London for years.

He rode out through the gate and followed the Shoreditch road north. He could see the Theatre through the trees and longed to turn into Holywell Street and ride past the Burbage house to the stage door. But it was too early for the actors to be there, and if he waited he would only interfere with the morning rehearsal. It would be better to write and thank them for the dagger, fastened so safely to his belt, although even if he had Mr. Shakespeare's way with words he would never be able to tell them what it meant to him.

It was no use, in any case, stretching out the good-bys. It only made it harder to leave. Robin touched his heel to the horse, and this time he did not look back.

All morning, as he rode north, he thought about London and his friends, but it was clear that Ruff was not thinking about London at all. He raced through the wild flowers by the side of the road, chasing imaginary rabbits and wild with excitement at being out in the country again. Ruff was a full-grown dog now, but he was behaving like a puppy.

There was one good thing, at least, about going back to Suffolk. A spaniel like Ruff was really better off in the country.

Robin did not stop for dinner, since Mrs. Heminges had given him a meat pie and some apples to take with him. He chewed as he rode along, sitting loose in the saddle and looking about him at the spring countryside.

It was a beautiful day, the sky cloudless and the grass starred with flowers. Robin did not know much about poetry but he remembered some lines he had once heard in the Theatre. He had liked them immediately, and even better when he had found out they were Mr. Shakespeare's.

> When daisies pied and violets blue
> And lady-smocks all silver-white
> And cuckoo-buds of yellow hue
> Do paint the meadows with delight . . .

Mr. Shakespeare knew a great deal about the country. They had talked about farming once and he had told Robin about a book written by a Dutchman who had some new ideas about feeding turnips to cattle. It sounded queer to feed roots to cows, but if Mr. Shakespeare said it would work it was probably worth trying.

Robin met several droves of pigs on their way south to the London market, and he looked at them with interest. They were fine animals, with their neat hoofs and fat sides, and Robin remembered that he had always liked pigs. The farmers in his part of Suffolk were not much interested in pigs, and yet they were an excellent investment.

The local farmers had their barley in, he noticed, and it was already pricking through the dark earth. It looked like a good year for farming. Robin began to whistle a little, because the day was so fine and the crops were going to be good. He found himself wondering how the lambing had gone this year at home.

He stopped before sundown at an inn whose great swinging sign was decorated with a picture of an oak tree. An ostler sprang forward to take his horse, and Robin lingered briefly to make sure that the rubbing down was done properly. Then he and Ruff walked into the main room of the inn, a handsome place with its leaded windows and striped cushions. Robin stretched out his feet comfortably while he and Ruff waited for their suppers. Afterward he went to bed between clean linen sheets by candlelight and could not help enjoying the sense of being grown-up and sleeping by himself in an inn.

He awoke to an uncomfortable feeling of loneliness and set himself to thinking of pigs again. Pigs seemed to be a calming sort of subject.

Robin set his route through Colchester, because he wanted to see the girl who had given him the buttered bun. He found she had gone away to be married, and after some difficulty he was able to get her married name and her address. There was no time to visit her and probably she would not wish him to, but Robin decided to send her something from Suffolk as a wedding present. There were a great many things made of silver around the house that no one ever seemed to use.

Robin spent the night in Colchester, and the people at the inn put up a packet of food that he ate the following noon for his dinner. He sat on the grass by the side of the road, holding the horse's reins, and a large frog hopped by and stopped to look at him. It was a handsome frog, chestnut color on top and yellow underneath, with scarlet spots, and Robin had never seen one like it anywhere except in Suffolk.

A thought struck him and he hailed a farmer who was creaking by with his oxen. The farmer said, with some contempt, that of course he was in Suffolk.

Robin drew a deep breath.

If he took one of the roads that led due north instead of going through Ipswich, he could be home by nightfall. He had no real reason for spending the night in Ipswich. His eldest aunt was not going to be any more forgiving tomorrow than she was tonight, and the best thing to do was to get the whole thing over as soon as possible. Then he could stop thinking about it.

Robin mounted and set his course for the north at the next fork in the road. The horse broke into a brisk trot and would have been delighted to canter if Robin had been willing. But Robin was not in such a hurry as all that. He felt that if he arrived just at suppertime, perhaps he could take his place quietly at the table and nothing would be said.

The landscape began to turn into the familiar one of his childhood, the gentle rolling country that was lovelier than ever in its spring green. They must have been having good weather, for everything looked very prosperous. All that might be a help. Aunt Isabella managed the farm accounts, and the steward and bailiff along with them, and if everything was going especially well she might feel less interest in the sins of her errant nephew.

Robin passed the old stone tower where the white owls sometimes nested, the one he had thought was haunted when he was a little boy. A succession of inquisitive small faces began to pop up behind the fences and hedgerows to look at him, but when he reined in to speak to the children they giggled and fled.

He circled the village because he did not have time to stop and greet everyone he might meet, but the children must have passed the word along that he had come home. The villagers hurried out into the common fields to wave to him, and when he waved back they set up a jubilant shout. He smiled at them, swinging his cap over his head, although it was not clear to him what they were so pleased about.

He did not rein in until he had reached the long line of oaks that led to the main entrance of the house. Last September Robin had planted some wild strawberry roots under one of the trees, and he could not help wondering if they had survived the winter.

They had, and were flourishing, their white and gold flowers just beginning to open among the jagged green leaves. Robin could see a few wisps of straw still clinging about the roots, so someone must have taken the trouble to cover them. That had been very kind.

He rode up the long avenue of oaks and his throat felt dry. He had the same hollow feeling he had known his first time on the stage, and although he took several deep breaths they did not help him very much.

Perhaps his Aunt Isabella was away for the day and not expected home until tomorrow. She did that sometimes. Robin was not so worried about Aunt Bertha and Aunt Eleanor; he was sure he could get on friendly terms with them if he were given a little time. It was Aunt Isabella that frightened him.

He gently touched the little dagger in his belt, for reassurance and to remind himself of the friends who had given it to him.

The villagers must have sent word to the servants that he was home again because they were lined up outside the front door, all bowing. He had not realized there were so many of them. He found he could not even remember all their names, although he did the best he could.

He entered the great hall and there were still more servants there, down to the cooks with their aprons and the excited kitchen boys. Old Martin stepped forward and bowed.

"The ladies are in the parlor, Sir Robert. They are waiting for you."

He drew a deep breath. He had a kind of sinking feeling inside of him; and perhaps it would have been wiser to stop somewhere for supper before he came. However, it was too late now.

"Thank you," he said, opened the parlor door and went inside.

Chapter 20

His three aunts were there to receive him, all in black and all standing erect. Their faces did not look welcoming.

Robin stood in the doorway and his heart failed him. He was glad, at least, that he had left Ruff outside.

Aunt Eleanor put her hand against the back of the embroidery frame, as if to steady herself, and it occurred to Robin that perhaps they were feeling just as nervous as he was. They looked older than he had remembered them, standing there in the black gowns that must have been fashionable in the previous reign, and they had never had any fun. They had never gone to a show, or visited a zoo, or been on a picnic, or walked home singing in the moonlight, and it suddenly seemed to Robin rather unfair. He had gone away and left them alone to a long winter in the old house, and from what he remembered of past winters it was not to be wondered that they looked a little gray and withdrawn. They had a right to be angry with him, and the sooner he made his peace the better.

He walked over to his Aunt Isabella, both because she was the eldest and because she looked the most forbidding. He took her gently by the shoulders, and they felt almost as frail as the small body of a bird under the heavy black material of her gown. She stiffened, whether with anger or surprise he did not know, and he kissed her full on the mouth.

He had to bend down a little to do it, since he had grown

taller during the winter. But it was a good kiss. He had learned that at least in London, where people did not mind showing that they loved each other. And he really did love his aunt, whether she loved him or not.

He kissed her again, just to make sure she had understood, and then he turned to Aunt Bertha.

Aunt Bertha was standing with her mouth open. She had a round little face, and she looked rather like Seena at the moment. Robin had never seen her look surprised before, since Aunt Bertha was usually the placid one. He put his arms around her and hugged her thoroughly, to show he was sorry he had given her any cause for worry.

At this point Aunt Eleanor abandoned her grip on the embroidery frame. "Oh, Robert!" she said, and burst into tears. She ran to him with her arms out and buried her face in his neck.

He stood there, holding the two of them in his arms and

murmuring comforting remarks, and over the tops of their heads he looked at his eldest aunt. She was still standing where he had left her, and there was an odd expression on her face. It was not disapproving exactly. It looked almost amused. It reminded Robin of the way Mrs. Knell had looked at him the first time he brought in the wood.

He felt an impulse to try an experiment. He winked at her.

Aunt Isabella stared at him for a long moment. Then her lips curled slightly and she almost smiled. When she spoke, however, her voice was as cool and correct as ever.

"Did you bring the dog back with you?" she asked. It was the first remark she had made.

"I did," said Robin agreeably. "I left him just outside in the hall."

He disentangled himself from the clinging arms of his two relatives and went to open the door. Ruff was sitting waiting, very alert, and he walked in with his tail waving. He looked very much at home.

Aunt Bertha reached out cautiously to pat him. "He is a fine dog," she said, and Robin remembered that she was the one who always introduced little animals into her embroidery designs.

"I dislike dogs around the house," said Aunt Isabella. She said it merely as one who states a fact.

"He is not dogs in general," said Robin. "He is only one spaniel. And he won't be around the whole house. He is used to sleeping with me."

Aunt Isabella looked at him. "And you apparently intend to have him go on sleeping with you."

"Yes," said Robin.

"You like your own way, don't you?" she said, and again she almost smiled.

"It is a kind of family failing," said Robin, smiling also.

"You are quite right," said Aunt Isabella. "We share it." She paused. "I cannot say that I shall ever bring myself to like your dog, Robert, but I will try to cultivate good relations with the animal since he belongs to you."

Robin bowed to her. "Aunt Isabella," he said, "I chose wisely when I chose you for my aunt."

"You remind me of your father," she remarked. "He was given to making pretty speeches also. I did not believe them then, and I do not believe them now. But I do not deny it is a pleasure to hear them." She really smiled this time, and for a moment her strong, clever face looked like a young girl's. Robin felt a strong impulse to kiss her again, and he did so.

"Where did you learn manners like that?" Aunt Isabella demanded. She had drawn back but she did not look seriously displeased.

"In London," said Robin.

"It must be an impulsive sort of town," she said dryly.

"It is a good town," said Robin. "You would like it." This was not said merely out of politeness. He was suddenly sure she would. At the supper table he would tell them about London.

Supper was served in the great hall, now that Robin was back, and there was an array of silver dishes in his honor. Everything was hot and very lavish, and Robin found he was hungry. He ate steadily while his aunts told him all the local news. There had been some difficulty with bats in the kitchen chimney, and January lightning had burned up one of the hayricks. The vicar's Christmas sermon had been most inspiring. The grandchild that old Martin had been waiting for turned out to be twins, a boy and a girl, and Robin said he would go and visit them the first thing in the morning.

Over the cheese and fruit, Robin told them in turn about London. He did not mention the Theatre, since he suspected this was a subject he had better work into gradually; but he described to his aunts the size and greatness of the city and he told them all about the Heminges family.

Aunt Isabella said she would like to meet Mrs. Heminges.

"We could all ride down to London in the autumn," said Robin. "Christmas is a busy season for them, but late October would be fine and a good time for traveling. While we are there I can show you St. Paul's Cathedral and the Royal Exchange. And I haven't visited the tombs in Westminster Abbey yet myself."

Aunt Bertha clasped her hands together, like a child who has been given a Christmas pie. Then she turned and looked doubtfully at Aunt Isabella.

"Don't look at me," said Aunt Isabella. "George's son is the head of the house."

"We could have a good time in London," said Robin. "The four of us together."

"I expect we could," Aunt Isabella admitted. "You are so firm about it that I doubt if we should dare to have anything else."

Robin grinned. He felt he would enjoy showing his Aunt Isabella around.

They lingered around the table, talking, until the servants lighted the silver candles and Ruff went to sleep with his nose on Robin's shoe. Robin picked him up gently, kissed his aunts good night and went up to bed. Everything was just as he had left it in his familiar room, except that someone had put a bowl of flowers on the small chest that held his schoolbooks and a spring night was outside the open window.

Ruff padded around the room with deep interest, looking

at everything, and Robin knew he would be happy in the country. Tomorrow he would take him out to see the twins and the new colt and all the lambs. He could also take him for a run across country, since Aunt Isabella had asked Robin to try out a mare she had just bought.

Robin decided he had better get himself a new pair of riding boots. His old ones would be too small for him now, and so would everything else he owned. He would send one of the grooms back to London, leading the horse that had been hired and carrying Robin's letters, and make up a shopping list to send along with him. He would send Martin's son and give him exact instructions about the best shops, along with an extra shilling to buy something for the twins.

One thing that Robin wanted in London was a copy of the book about turnips that Mr. Shakespeare had recommended. It was called *The Four Books of Husbandry*, and if it turned out that the Dutchman was right about turnips it would make a great difference to the Wakefield cattle. There was never enough hay for the whole herd by the end of winter, but if they could eat stored roots the problem would be solved. If it worked in the Low Countries, it might very well work in England. He would talk it over with his Aunt Isabella as soon as he had the printed word to support him. Perhaps he could give her the book as a present and they could read it together.

His other aunts might like presents, too. There had been a little fan at the Royal Exchange, of swansdown with seed pearls on it, that Aunt Eleanor would like, and for Aunt Bertha a bracelet of coral. He did not want to give them anything dark-colored or practical. They had plenty of practical things.

There was something he wanted for himself, too, something that only cost sixpence and would fit easily into the saddlebag of Martin's son. It was the pamphlet that had been printed of *Romeo and Juliet*. The company had discussed the idea of putting out a corrected version, but Robin did not want to wait for it. He wanted to read it over again now, and perhaps when Aunt Isabella had finished the Dutch book she might like to hear about her nephew's first appearance as an actor.

Robin climbed into bed and Ruff settled down in his usual place on the floor by his side. Robin leaned out to give him a final pat on the head, as he always did the last thing at night, and then he said his prayers and blew out the candle.

Outside the window were the stars, with the leaves of his favorite oak laced in front of them. For a moment he lay looking at them, and then he turned over with a comfortable sigh and promptly fell asleep.

Sir Robert Wakefield was home again.

Author's Note

The actors mentioned in this book were all real people, and so were their families and apprentices; and the reader might like to know what happened to them afterward.

The Heminges family went on living in the same street and kept on having children until there were fourteen in all. Thomasina, who is called Seena in the story, married an actor in the company. John Heminges lived to be very old, and in his will he asked to be buried near "my loving wife Rebecca" and under the same stone if possible.

The Burbage brothers were not able to get a new lease for the land on which the Theatre was built. So they came with a carpenter and a wrecking crew and pulled the building down. They carried all the timber across the Thames and put it together again as a new theatre which they called the Globe. Five other actors in the company helped to lease the land for the Globe and put up the building—John Heminges, William Shakespeare, Augustine Phillips, William Kempe and Thomas Pope.

Most of the actors lived near the Globe, and even Shakespeare stayed there for a time. Then he moved over to the west side of London and took lodgings near the Heminges family. Thomas Pope went on adopting children who were cared for by his housekeeper, and in his will he left her all his rings except the opal one. Augustine Phillips, who eventually had five children, made special mention in his will of

Samuel Gilburne, leaving his former apprentice "my mouse-colored velvet hose and a white taffety doublet, a black taffety suit, my purple cloak, sword and dagger and my bass viol." He remembered Shakespeare in the same will and left twenty shillings in gold to Alexander Cooke.

Cooke, who is called Sandy in this story, also went to live near the Globe. He named his elder daughter Rebecca, and when he died he left his four children to the care of John Heminges and a close friend of Heminges named Henry Condell.

Henry Condell was an important actor in the same company and brought up his nine children near the Heminges family in the parish of St. Mary Aldermanbury. He and Heminges outlived everyone else in the original company. They were afraid that Shakespeare's plays might become lost and so they brought out a complete collection of them which is known as the First Folio. They did it, they said, not to get money or fame but "only to keep the memory of so worthy a friend and fellow alive as was our Shakespeare."